D1577130

C153398860

# Kid Dynamite

Sent from the safety of the distant East, government agent Scott Taylor arrives at Adobe Wells. His mission is to tackle the corruption which is rife in the arid landscape in which he finds himself.

But Cody Carter has other plans. He has ruled Franklin County for years with his own small army of outlaws and has bribed displaced Cheyenne warriors to do his killing for him. Notified of the coming of Taylor by a well-paid spy in Washington DC, Carter sends out his top gunman to stop the agent.

Scott has no idea Kid Dynamite is waiting to kill him in his own evil way and it looks as if he is doomed.

# Kid
# Dynamite

## MICHAEL D. GEORGE

**A Black Horse Western**

ROBERT HALE · LONDON

© Michael D. George 2008
First published in Great Britain 2008

ISBN 978-0-7090-8639-0

Robert Hale Limited
Clerkenwell House
Clerkenwell Green
London EC1R 0HT

www.halebooks.com

Typeset by
Derek Doyle & Associates, Shaw Heath
Printed and bound in Great Britain by
CPI Antony Rowe, Chippenham, Wiltshire

*Dedicated with gratitude to the doctors
and nursing staff of The Princess of Wales Hospital
for saving my life.*

# PROLOGUE

It snorted and moved like a mythical beast through the darkness into the light of the small railhead town. Steam hissed like a million sidewinders as the engineer brought the mighty locomotive to a grinding halt. This was the furthest south any of the railroad companies had ever ventured in their bid to get closer to the vast cattle ranches which occupied this otherwise desolate place. Stockpens were filled with longhorns ready to be loaded into the specially constructed cars behind the engine and its tender.

Men moved from the lantern-lit buildings to greet the long line of sidecars. Each carried a grappling hook and a lantern and knew his job. They moved between the pens to the cars and started their work.

Only the last car was meant for something other than filling with prime beef on the hoof. Its sliding doors opened and a tall lean man looked out at

7

the busy scene. Holding the reins of his horse in his gloved right hand he dropped to the ground, then encouraged his big gelding to follow him. The animal was nervous as it was led through the row of pens filled with snorting steers.

The horse did not relax until its master reached a line of wooden buildings some distance from the doomed animals. The man pulled on his top coat in a vain attempt to hold the night chill at bay, then he waited. His eyes observed rather than saw. They were trained to study everyone and everything.

The tall man sucked the last of the smoke from his cigarette. He was about to drop it on to the sand at his feet when he saw the shadow of a rider stretched out across the ground beside a building to his left. He remained quite still. As the horse was steered around a corner and headed straight for him, he did not flinch. He simply watched.

The rider was a cavalry officer. He eased his mount up to the tall figure, who was still holding his reins, then halted. For a few seconds neither man spoke. They just looked at one another as though absorbing every detail.

'It's dark,' the officer said.

'It'll get lighter,' the tall man replied.

The officer smiled. 'Major Taylor?'

'Yep!'

There were no more words. The officer looked

all around to ensure that they were not being watched, then he pulled out a sealed envelope from his left gauntlet and handed it to the figure below him. A swift salute and the cavalryman was gone.

Scott Taylor opened the envelope. It was in code but that was no problem. He digested the few words and nodded to himself. He pulled a match from his vest pocket, struck it and lit the paper. He did not drop it until it was nothing more than embers. His narrowed eyes watched as the gentle night breeze blew the ashes away.

He had just been given his next orders.

He was about to remount when something alerted his honed senses. A sound to his right made him turn round sharply. He saw the gun first and then its owner. A shot blasted out. Its deafening sound echoed around the railhead as its white lightning hurtled towards him. The bullet caught the side wall of the nearby building. A thousand splinters showered over both man and horse. Taylor kept hold of his reins with his left hand as his right drew one of his matched Colts from its holster.

In one fluid action he returned fire.

His bullet found its mark. He watched as the man staggered and then fell into the sand. Without checking whether his attacker were alive or dead Taylor holstered his weapon and threw himself on to his saddle.

Before anyone could reach the fallen man the rider was gone.

Dust swirled across the flat, desolate plain as the morning sun evaporated the night's frost. A haze of enervating heat rose from the solid ground as the rider came into view and aimed his lathered-up mount due south. The emptiness stretched out for what seemed miles as he continued to spur and spur. There was an urgency in his wrists as he whipped the horse with the long ends of his reins. He seemed to be either unable or simply unwilling to allow his mount to rest. He was a driven man who was on a mission that only he could accomplish.

There had already been one attempt on his life. He knew it would not be the last.

For the rider was a man who had been assigned by the highest of authorities to solve a riddle which the local law seemed unable to fathom. The rider knew that there had to be corruption somewhere in this riddle.

There was a feeling among those who had sent this tall, lean man to the arid Arizona Territories that they would never set eyes upon him again. He had not been the first whom they had persuaded to volunteer for this mission. The others had all disappeared without trace.

Was this a suicide mission? A job which was just

too big for any one man to handle? There were many who thought so. Many who believed that there were just some places in the Wild West that could never be tamed.

They also believed that there were some outlaws who could never be captured or brought to justice. But no matter how bad the odds, a few brave men tried their best to do just that.

Scott Taylor was such a man. Taylor had once served with distinction in the Union army during the war and had reached the rank of major before the hostilities ended. Following that he had become a renowned United States marshal in the Midwest. His record was unequalled. Few could match his honesty, loyalty or courage.

It was only when he reached the age of thirty-two that his talents had been called upon by the secret service. They wanted someone who was trustworthy and had the ability to survive in the most dangerous of situations.

A man who could be relied upon to risk everything to bring outlaws to justice or take on entire gangs if that was what was required. If it said 'dead or alive' on the Wanted posters Taylor would try his best to achieve the latter. However, he would and could dispatch most gunfighters with his pair of trusty matched Colt .45s.

He had the ability to perform what was required of him. To play the fool or pretend to be a wanted outlaw just like those he hunted came as second nature to the rider. Yet those who had recruited Taylor had not given him any identification papers or silver stars to show his authority.

Should he be discovered there was no one he could turn to in order to save his hide.

Scott Taylor was alone.

He was also in a hurry. The desert started to heat up and the sun grew more ferocious with every passing minute. The rider knew that he had to reach the small isolated fortress called Fort Briggs before the day was much older.

Taylor could see the scattered remnants of bleached bones as he thundered along. Some were easily identifiable as animal but there were others which were more chilling. He knew that some wagon trains had once wrongly thought this was a safe route to California. All they found was thirst and ultimately death.

Taylor dragged his reins to his chest. The high purple mesas seemed never to get any closer, no matter how far he rode into this land designed by Satan himself.

At last the horseman dropped to the ground. He held the reins in one hand and placed his Stetson on the sand with the other. He plucked one of his canteens from the saddle horn and unscrewed its stopper. He poured the entire contents into the crown of his hat and watched as the horse drank.

He contented himself with the few drops of water which remained in the canteen, then hung the empty container back on the saddle horn. He shook the others. They were now all empty.

Taylor had hoped to have reached his destination before the water had run out. Having never been to this land before he had miscalculated how much of the precious liquid he would require to reach Fort Briggs.

The animal finished the water and then pushed the hat around with its nose, vainly seeking more to quench its thirst. Taylor stooped and plucked it back up. He ran fingers through his hair, then placed it back on his head. The dampness felt cool. He sighed, rubbed his eyes and then stepped back into his stirrup. He was sore but ignored his pain. He gathered the reins in his gloved hands and then spurred again.

If there was one thing the army had taught him it was how to navigate across the most hostile of landscapes. He could not see it but knew that Fort Briggs was in the direction he was riding.

He spurred even harder and hung on.

The horse had consumed the last of the water. Now it had to repay its master and reach the fortress so that he could get himself a drink.

There were at least three hours before the sun reached its zenith and made the desert a place where only sidewinders could survive.

Scott Taylor rode on along the trail once used by the wagon trains. The grooves of their metal wheel rims were still carved into the ground.

Suddenly out of the corner of his left eye he saw something catching the sun. A fleeting flash of light drew his attention as he drove his horse on. He focused and saw the flash again from a rise between himself and a towering mesa.

For a split second his weary mind tried to think what it was, then he saw the distant puff of gunsmoke. Sand kicked up ahead of him as the powerful buffalo-gun shell hit the ground. Then he heard the sound which mimicked thunder. It could not keep up with the speed of the bullet.

Taylor dragged the horse to a standstill and leapt off the saddle. He grabbed the reins tightly in both hands and pulled the animal down until it lay on the sand.

Another bullet from the powerful weapon passed over him, quickly followed by the noise of the hammer hitting the firing pin.

Taylor held his nervous horse in check. His eyes screwed up as they desperately tried to locate the man with the huge gun. He saw the light catch the telescopic sights and ducked.

A mighty explosion erupted a dozen yards behind the man and his horse. Heat and debris spat over them. The ground shook as though a giant had stomped upon it. A fiery ton of sand blew up into the air and fell heavily over both horse and rider.

Taylor knew that the dynamite had been buried on the trail by someone capable of igniting it from distance with deadly shooting accuracy.

To his knowledge there was only one man who chose this form of execution.

Taylor calmed the terrified horse and peered up over the sand. He saw the disappearing silhouette of a man riding away and although they had never met, he instantly knew who it was.

It was the man whom Scott Taylor had been warned about. A notorious outlaw in his early twenties who was an expert with explosives and also a deadly shot. He was thought to be named William Hartman.

More commonly known as Kid Dynamite.

# ONE

The mysterious and ruthless Kid Dynamite had made his presence known a dozen or more miles behind the thundering hoofs of Scott Taylor's exhausted mount. The secret service man had been warned about the young outlaw's ability and cunning when it came to the creative and destructive use of the deadly explosive sticks that he favoured. Taylor had not thought that the Kid would get so close, though. His ears were still ringing with the painful thunder of exploding dynamite.

Since driving on Taylor had made sure that he did not keep to the grooved wagon-wheel tracks as he had done earlier. Now he made sure that he gave them a wide berth. The outlaw might have repeated his devilish ploy and planted even more sticks of dynamite close to the well-defined ruts cut into the sun-baked ground.

Unlike so many men cut from the same cloth as

16

the ex-soldier, Taylor had the ability to learn by his mistakes. He had come close to getting himself blown into a million bits and had silently vowed it would not happen again.

With every stride of the tall bay gelding Taylor kept searching the unfamiliar terrain for a hint of the presence of the ruthless man. He had actually thought him to be an invention of those who had sent him to this desolate place.

He knew that most men armed with a long-barrelled single-shot buffalo-gun would simply lie in wait and shoot their chosen target off the back of his horse.

But not Kid Dynamite.

The Kid seemed to relish the game. The thrill of blasting his enemies into countless pieces rather than just shooting them appeared to be his favourite ploy. It was obvious to the experienced rider that the Kid was addicted to dynamite, just like those who were entranced by fire and became arsonists.

Taylor whipped his reins for the umpteenth time. He was wondering how Kid Dynamite knew of his arrival and his route. There was only one explanation: someone back East had given or sold the information.

Someone who was in the pay of the dubious souls who ruled this territory as though it belonged to them.

The rider knew his mission was doomed to failure on a dozen levels yet he had chosen to accept it. Taylor was not easily scared. Even when outnumbered, he did not flinch from what he regarded as his duty.

He was working for the government for the betterment of his fellow Americans. He knew that few would ever know of the risks he and his fellow agents would take in order to achieve their goals but that made no difference.

Taylor rode on.

The threads of the story he had been given wove through his mind. He wondered which of the men who had sent him here had actually betrayed him.

It seemed impossible that any of them had. Yet there was no other way that the outlaw could have known. Someone in the heart of the secret service was in the pay of the very men he had come to try and arrest.

If Kid Dynamite knew the exact date, time and trail he was taking then it followed that the outlaw knew more. He knew where he was meant to go and why. Taylor wondered whether the young outlaw might also know whom he was meant to meet at Fort Briggs. Josh Morgan had, like Taylor himself, been an officer in the Union army and was one of the few souls he'd been told he could trust with his life. Taylor had only learned of Morgan when he had arrived at the Adobe Wells railhead and disembarked from the freight train.

A cavalry officer had given him the sealed orders naming Morgan as the man he had to meet at Fort Briggs. Apart from that Taylor knew nothing of the remainder of his task. Again, sealed orders were going to reveal what he had to do next.

Taylor could not shake the thoughts from his mind.

How much did the gang know? Was his every move already in the hands of Kid Dynamite and those he worked for?

The thought chilled Taylor. Even in this satanic land where men melted under the hot blazing sun he felt a cold sweat trace his spine.

Taylor was no coward but he was also no fool. If everything he was meant to achieve had been compromised he had to change the plans and find his own way of bettering his foes.

A few miles further on it became obvious that the lethal outlaw was no longer anywhere around. He must have fallen back to a better place to ambush or kill, Taylor told himself.

Taylor looked through the shimmering heat and caught sight of the distant fortress. He wondered if that was where Kid Dynamite might have retreated to. Where more sticks of explosives could have been planted to greet him. There was only one way to find out.

He spurred.

The fort had been abandoned years earlier by a government unable to afford its upkeep at the height of the war. Yet it still stood defiantly battling against the elements. It remained as a reminder of a time when a thousand troops were stationed within its wooden-walled precincts. The rider no longer had to spur his mount, the animal could smell the water inside the walls of weathered tree-trunks.

Taylor hung on as the horse went through the open gates, which seemed to have been damaged in some battle long since. He headed straight to the well and its overflowing water troughs. He dismounted and brushed the dust from his trail clothes as the horse drank its fill beside him.

Taylor pulled the small leather loops off his gun hammers and rested a hand upon one of the grips. Should trouble start once more, he was ready.

His gaze darted around the wooden buildings all about him in search of the man he had come to meet. He also looked for any signs of others who might have come to this place in search of sanctuary, salvation or just plain murder.

There was no sign of anyone, but someone had been here.

Taylor knew that the troughs had not filled themselves. Not in this hot climate. They had been filled recently, otherwise the precious liquid would have evaporated.

He walked to the well and started to hoist the bucket from the water far below. It took nearly a minute before he set eyes upon it and its clear contents. Taylor placed the bucket on the well wall, removed his gloves, tucked them into his gunbelt and cupped his hands.

The water tasted good. He ran his wet hands over his neck and then looked around the deserted fort again.

His orders had been to meet a man called Josh Morgan. Morgan was said to be nearly fifty with snow-white hair. He, like Taylor, had been recruited by the authorities. Also like Taylor, he was a law unto himself.

Taylor tied the reins of his horse to a hitching rail and started to walk towards the stables. They were extensive, stretching the entire length of the east wall. It was obvious that at one time a huge number of horses had been stabled there.

As he entered the long building he felt a cold chill wash over him. The shade felt good. It was the first he had experienced since leaving the train at Adobe Wells three days earlier.

Taylor paused.

There were no horses in the stables.

Taylor walked along the length of the open-fronted structure until he saw the fresh horse-droppings. They were nearly dry but they indicated that someone had been here recently.

Taylor wondered whether it had been Morgan who had stabled his mount here, or someone else. It seemed doubtful that anyone else would seek out this remote fort unless they knew of its supply of cool water.

Then he recalled Kid Dynamite. Had it been he who had left his horse inside these stables? The question bothered him. It had no answer.

Taylor pulled out a cigar. He placed it in the corner of his mouth and then found a match. He struck it and sucked in its flame. The smoke felt good.

If Josh Morgan had been here, Taylor thought, where had he gone?

And why?

If it had been the outlaw, had the Kid set traps?

He inhaled the smoke even more deeply into his lungs, as if it could answer the questions his tired mind kept posing. He strolled back out into the sun. It was like entering an oven.

He bit his lip and continued to walk. This time he was headed to the troopers' and officers' quarters.

After more than an hour of fruitless search Taylor confirmed that he was totally alone in the deserted fortress. He filled his canteens, then unsaddled his mount. The animal was exhausted as it ate the grain he had poured on to the ground from his saddlebags.

Taylor knew that he was stuck in this place until his horse recovered from the long hard ride. That would not be until the next day at the earliest. He studied the fort walls and the parapet which ran along the top of its four sides.

With his long legs he was able to ascend two steps at a time until he reached the high parapet. His eyes studied the dry land that encircled the small army outpost. The mesas seemed to be miles away. How close they truly were he did not know. Taylor had never been to this territory before and his ignorance troubled him.

In all his days he had always had some knowledge of his surroundings in order to fight his corner. Death came swiftly to the unprepared.

Arizona had so far been unlike anywhere else that he had ever visited and he knew that it held dangers of which he was ignorant. Ignorance could cost you the ultimate price. He recalled the battlefields he had fought upon and the bodies of so many ignorant souls which littered them.

He tapped the ash from his cigar and walked along the three-foot-wide platform. He kept a steady pace as his eyes watched the distant horizon through the shimmering haze. His instincts warned him to be wary.

Just when he had almost completed a full circuit of the high parapet something caught his eye.

He stopped.

Taylor rubbed his chin and screwed up his eyes. He threw the cigar away. The heat haze made it hard to see clearly but he tried all the same. Something out there had alerted his honed senses. It was something that he had never witnessed before and for a moment he did not understand what he was looking at.

Then he realized what it was.

A cold chill swept over him.

Smoke signals twisted up in calculated plumes into the blue cloudless sky from one of the high mesas.

'Indians!' Taylor muttered to himself. He lowered his head and gave out a long sigh before returning his gaze to the terrifying spectacle. If there was one thing Scott Taylor had absolutely no knowledge of, it was Indians of any description.

'Damn it all!'

# TWO

There was no time to think. Pure survival instinct was now commanding the ex-military man's every action. Taylor ran to the edge of the wooden walk-way, ran helter-skelter down the stairs from the high parapet to the sand and moved to the huge damaged gates. They were barely hanging on their hinges but Taylor knew that they were vital if he were to be attacked. They had to create a barrier that might buy him a little extra time.

Being from far to the east he had never even set eyes upon a real Indian. Wooden effigies outside cigar stores and the crude drawings on the covers of dime novels barely came close to anything remotely lifelike. But the stories, both true and false, fuelled his fertile imagination.

Taylor rested a shoulder against one of the massive gates and tried to push it back to where it belonged. After a few moments he did manage to force its hefty bulk across the soft sand until it filled half the gaping gap in the fortress wall.

It was unsteady and rocked but at least it was where it was meant to be.

The second half of the once impressive gates proved more of a problem, though. It leaned over at such a precarious angle that he could not budge it. Only the bottom hinge was attached to the wall and that looked as though it would give way at any moment, letting the gate crash on to the sand.

It appeared to be an impossible chore but Taylor did not quit so easily. The ex-soldier had faced many challenges in his time and always managed to get the better of them. A stubborn streak in him had saved his hide on more than one occasion and he trusted it would do so again. There was always a way around any problem, Taylor thought to himself, you just had to be able to see it.

For a few fleeting moments he stood and gasped as he tried to drag air into his lungs whilst his mind raced for a feasible solution. Then his attention fell on his saddle. It lay on the ground beside the water troughs.

He snapped his fingers.

'Yeah! That might just work!' Taylor said aloud. 'There's only one way to find out!'

Taylor ran to it and untied the cutting rope from the saddle horn. He began to uncoil the fifty-foot length and made his way back to the swaying gates. He pulled his gloves on to his hands again, then tied the end of the rope around the top of the gate. Using all his strength he tightened the knot, held the loose rope in his hands and raced up the steps to the high platform again.

He looped the rope around the long signboard with the faded fort name painted upon its surface, then wrapped it around his shoulders and waist. He flexed his muscles and began to walk back down the steps towards the ground, feeding the rope around his ample frame as he went. He had become a human lever. He was using his weight to lift the heavy gate.

Slowly but surely the gate rose off the sand. By the time he had reached the fortress floor it was upright. Swaying, but upright all the same.

Taylor moved cautiously towards the wall whilst keeping a firm grip on the rope. With every step he pulled in the slack until none remained.

Sweat burned his screwed-up eyes as he held the gate in check. Filling his lungs with the hot desert air, he carried on with the Herculean task. His skilled hands tied the rope off around the solid base of the wooden steps. He then moved to the gates and pushed them back into place. Last of all he found a long plank of lumber, dragged it across the sun-drenched courtyard and propped it up between the two gates, making them as one.

Taylor was exhausted but still managed to force himself back up to the high platform. He rested both gloved hands upon the top of the gates and stared out to the smoke signal. It was still rising threateningly from the mesa. Still sending unknown messages.

Then, as he turned, he spotted more smoke. Another set of Indian signals was rising heavenward from a high ridge at least ten miles away from the mesa.

'Damn!' Taylor cussed. 'What the hell have I gotten myself tangled up in?'

He rubbed his dry mouth along the back of his sleeve. He was surrounded by walls made from tree trunks. Taylor had never seen so much wood in any one place before.

It did not make him feel any safer. It was like being trapped inside the biggest coffin in creation.

# THREE

San Remas was a small town barely within the unmarked borders of the vast untamed Arizona territory. To the uninitiated onlooker it could have passed for any of a score of similar settlements south of the border in the Mexican heartland. Sombreros still outnumbered Stetsons. Whitewashed adobes dominated but a few more American-style structures had been erected in recent years. Each with the same name upon its façade.

Carter.

There was a very good reason for that. Cody Carter had arrived with his impressive gang of fifteen gunfighters shortly before the border town had started to flourish. Without him it would more than likely have turned to dust like so many others and blown away into the surrounding desert

For Carter had a way of making money, either legally or illegally, it did not matter to the well-nourished man. It was said by those who knew him that Carter could corrupt a nun. Possibly even a bishop. Ordinary folk were just too naïve for his sort of person.

Carter was a man of many faces. He had been an elected Franklin County official for nearly a decade. He had been a ruthless criminal for far longer. His wealth was based on both occupations. Creative bookkeeping had always been his forte. Politics had secured him a federal budget and the ability to steal legally.

His criminal activities had blossomed as a result. For if there was one thing the vast territory offered an ambitious man, it was land. Land which was peppered with settlers but very little else apart from restless Indian tribes.

Like the majority of politicians everywhere he had discovered how easy it was to milk the innocent and honest of their cash in the name of innumerable taxes and fines.

Some said it was impossible to sneeze in Franklin County without incurring a fine.

In recent months Carter had also managed to find a most lucrative sideline.

This was one which was despised by all sane souls. Gun- and liquor-running to the Indians had proved to be his most lucrative business. Carter had befriended the various tribes who still clung to life in the vast wilderness. In truth he hated all of them, but it made good business sense to let the Cheyenne and their fellow tribes believe the opposite.

Especially if you wanted to stir up trouble with the settlers and become land rich, as Carter did. Indians plied with repeating rifles, unlimited ammunition and countless barrels of whiskey could cause a lot of trouble. They could do a lot of killing and leave a lot of vacant land ready to be purchased cheaply.

Carter had snapped up every one of the plots which had come on to the market after the Indians had done their worst. Some thought he was insane to buy land with blood upon its sand. They did not know the truth. Carter knew that by the time they did it would be too late to do anything about it.

Unlike those who had plied their trade in earlier days, Carter did not charge the Indians anything for the weapons and whiskey he provided.

He was their friend. Or so they believed. They would do anything for him. And did.

Cody Carter in turn could reap the rewards without any fear of the law pointing the finger in his direction. When you controlled a county government you controlled everything.

Including the law.

Carter was the law. Anyone foolish enough to disagree with any of his rulings soon discovered why he surrounded himself with fifteen top gunfighters.

Until now it had all run like a well-oiled machine. Outside interference had been dealt with by his henchmen. It would take an army to get the better of Carter and he knew that the war had ruled out any such possibility. Even Washington was cash strapped and could ill afford to waste money on mere territory disputes when real states had to be rebuilt.

Carter, a well-built man in his late forties, walked along the balcony of his home, newly constructed on the very edge of San Remas. He stared out at the dusty terrain and spotted the rider who, he knew, was one of the most dangerous creatures he had ever employed.

Carter sucked on his cigar and wondered why Kid Dynamite was riding in so fast. He knew that the youngster feared nothing, but the way he spurred his mount worried the businessman.

'Go down and see what's wrong with the Kid, Jacko!' Carter told his number one gun, Jackson Wright.

Wright touched his hat brim. 'Sure enough, boss.'

Carter remained on the balcony as the Kid dragged his reins back and leapt from his saddle. The Kid passed Wright halfway up the stairs as he raced to his employer.

'What's wrong, Kid?' Carter asked the panting youngster.

'Taylor's here!' came the reply.

'I thought I told you to kill him.'

'I tried but them Cheyenne started sending up smoke right behind me.' Kid Dynamite rubbed the trail dust from his youthful features and accepted the drink handed to him by the thoughtful Carter. He swilled it down in one shot. 'I managed to get a few shots at that secret service *hombre* but then I seen the smoke going up from Big Mesa.'

'Did it scare ya, Kid?' Wright asked as he caught up with the Kid.

Kid Dynamite gritted his teeth. If looks could kill, Jackson Wright would have been already on his way to Hell.

'Injuns don't scare me, Jacko. I just got me more sense than getting in their way when they're on the warpath.'

Carter pointed his cigar at the two men. 'The Kid's right. I told Chief Red Eagle to start a ruckus on them settlers down along Blood River a week or so back. He must have just gotten them Cheyenne bucks drunk enough to start it.'

The Kid leaned closer to Carter. 'Ya could have told me about that, boss. I might have lost my scalp out there.'

'You *were* scared.' Wright grinned widely.

Cody Carter walked between the best two of his

33

many henchmen just before they struck out at one another. He paused. They both held their fists in check and watched their overweight paymaster as he removed the cigar from his lips.

'Where was Taylor headed, Kid?'

'I figure he must have bin headed for the old fort, boss. I did manage to hit one of my dynamite sticks with the buffalo-gun before I lit out for here. There was the biggest damn blast ya ever did see!'

'Did it blow him up?'

'I ain't sure.' The Kid shrugged. 'It went kinda quiet after that and then I seen the smoke right behind me. I didn't have time to wait and see.'

'He was on the old wagon-train trail to Fort Briggs.' Carter nodded. Smoke enveloped his head for a few seconds. When it disappeared a smile was etched across the wrinkled face. 'Just like my informants told me. Good! That was money well spent. If Taylor's still alive then he's headed for the fort to meet up with another of them secret service men. Just like I was told.'

'Who's he gonna meet up with, boss?' Wright asked.

Carter shrugged and tapped the thick ash from his cigar before returning it to his teeth.

'I ain't sure of that. My contact back East didn't know the name of the varmint Taylor was told to meet up with.'

'Could it be someone from San Remas?'

Carter glanced at Wright again. 'Could be, Jacko. But who?'

'If my dynamite ain't done for him do ya reckon them Injuns will kill Taylor for us, boss?' Kid Dynamite questioned.

'The really interesting thing is that Fort Briggs is right between the Cheyenne's main camp and Blood River, boys.' Carter smiled. 'If that lousy government bastard gets in their way, he's a goner for sure. Red Eagle ain't the sort to take prisoners when he's fired up with red-eye.'

All three men laughed.

There was no humour in any of the bloodthirsty trio but they laughed all the same. They laughed loudly. It echoed all around San Remas.


The blazing afternoon sun burned through his shirt and vest into Scott Taylor's back as he checked his half-hunter pocket watch. It was nearly three and the afternoon was only halfway gone. Taylor returned the golden timepiece to his pants pocket and stared out at the smoke, which now came from three different locations. Salt stung his eyes like crazed hornets but he kept on looking at the terrifying apparition.

How did you fight them?

These were hitherto untried opponents for Taylor. He had read that Indians never attacked after dark but he did not know whether that was true. Was it, like so many other myths, just the creation of dime novelists who had never ventured further than the Hudson River? Even if it was true, sundown was still over four hours away.

Darkness would not save him today, he thought.

He walked slowly around the high parapet, cradling his Winchester across his chest. Sweat ran down his face from the hatband and dripped on to his bandanna. Taylor had been in many battles and fights over the years but none like this promised to be. He wiped the fear from his brow with his shirt-sleeve and tried to think.

Taylor paused.

He then noticed a small cloud of dust beyond the long ridge of hills. It rose high into the dry air and hung there like an eagle on a thermal.

Long before he saw them, he heard their war cries mixed with the sound of thundering hoofs.

His heart started to pound.

Then they appeared.

A long line of more than forty Cheyenne warriors sat astride their paint ponies. They all drew back their rope reins and stopped their mounts. Taylor had never seen so much colour before. The sun danced off the feathered war bonnets, gleaming rifle barrels and painted shields. No dime novelist had ever described this sight. If any had Taylor might never have ventured West.

There was a silence that was deafening. The Indians were watching the fort as Taylor in turn watched them. The Cheyenne sensed that Fort Briggs was no longer deserted.

Taylor ducked down and ran to the steps. He descended them three at a time until his boots hit the parade ground dust. Without actually knowing why, he was running toward the officers' quarters at full speed.

He raised a boot, kicked the door open and entered.

For a few moments he stood clawing at his thoughts. Then he recalled the rifles and boxes of ammunition he had seen there hours earlier. The score of Springfield single-shot rifles were racked and held in place by a chain and padlock. Taylor cranked his Winchester's hand guard, pulled back the trigger and fired.

The padlock shattered. The chain rattled, slid through all the rifles' straps and fell heavily to the floor.

Desperately, Taylor scooped up the rifles from the rack, then staggered back to the front gate. He laboured up the wooden steps and dropped all the weapons on the high platform.

Taylor turned and ran down the stairs to the ground. Again he sped back to the building as fast as his weary legs could carry him. Then he grabbed as many boxes of bullets as his hands could cope with and returned to the parapet.

He had a plan brewing in his brain.

It might be a long shot but it was his only chance. One man against at least forty were bad odds. He feverishly started to load each of the rifles.

It had to work. It just had to.

# FOUR

The Cheyenne were chanting at the wooden obstacle between Blood River and the settlers they had been primed with hard liquor to attack. They had spotted the repaired gates and caught a fleeting glimpse of someone on the high ramparts. Yet they were sure that there had to be more than one defiant man within the fortress. Their war cries grew louder as the whiskey did its worst.

Taylor was soaked in his own fear yet he did not rest. He knew that he might only have a few seconds before the entire line of Cheyenne warriors erupted into action and started down the ridge towards the fort.

He had faced many a cavalry charge during the war but none had filled him with as much trepidation as the one which was looming.

Taylor lifted a dozen of the loaded rifles and started to move along the parapet. Every two yards he propped one of the long-barrelled weapons between the pointed pine trunks and cocked its hammer. He did not pause until every one of the rifles rested in place along Fort Briggs's front wall. Staying low he returned to the boxes of cartridges and then placed them at ten feet intervals.

Taylor tossed his hat aside, knelt and peered over the wall at the braves. They were starting to make a lot more noise. The shrilling sound was something new to Taylor.

It clawed at his already frayed nerves.

The stories he had read about what Indians did to white men filled his mind. He prayed that none of them was true but feared that they were. He had seen what Yankees and Johnny Rebs could do to one another and they were meant to be civilized.

His heart raced.

The Indian with the largest, most impressive war bonnet brought his mount forward and started to wave his rifle at his braves. There was power in the warrior's gesture which struck a chord with Taylor. He had seen many a military leader do the same to soldiers both infantry and cavalry.

Taylor swallowed hard and bit his lip. His guts felt as though they had already been stuck with a knife.

'You don't want to attack me!' he mumbled at them. 'Go on! Ride around this fort and leave this soldier be!'

Even if they had been able to hear him, his words would have had no effect. The warriors were fired up with enough whiskey flowing through their veins to blind most men. In a way they were blind. Blind to what they were doing and why. Blind to the fact that they were being used. The brand-new rifles in their hands tipped the scales. After years of one broken treaty after another and forced from their ancestral lands to this desolate place, they wanted to fight. One white man had given them the ability to punish so many others.

The screams of the Cheyenne reached their highest pitch. Then, as one, they raised their rifles together and kicked their ponies into motion.

Dust spewed up from the unshod hoofs.

Taylor watched in terror as the entire line of Cheyenne started to charge down from the ridge. They astounded the experienced ex-cavalryman. He had never seen anyone able to control a horse with legs alone whilst riding bareback so that both hands were capable of using a repeating rifle. If they fought as well as they rode, Taylor knew that he was already a dead man.

The shots started to rain down on the fort. A thousand hornets could not have created such a din. Chunks of wood splattered up into the air from all along the wall as deadly lead cut into it.

It was relentless.

Kneeling like a man in prayer, Taylor moved

along the line of rifles. As he reached the first single-shot rifle he paused, aimed and fired, then moved on to the next one as quickly as he could. For every one shot he fired at least forty were returned.

Taylor wondered whether they believed that there was more than one solitary soul trapped inside Fort Briggs. Could he possibly fool them?

It was another unanswerable question.

By the time he had reached the last Springfield he had managed to hit at least five of the attacking braves, but now they were at the base of the wall. Taylor could see the gates being tested. They bulged inwards.

Somehow they held firm.

For the moment anyway.

Bullets tore up from the riders' rifles as the ponies milled around below Taylor's high vantage point. They were everywhere. Taylor heard the gates being forced again and again. He ran back to them along the high walkway as though his mere presence might stop the Cheyenne.

Once the gates gave way, he knew he would be finished. Somehow he had to delay the inevitable. Taylor had to buy himself precious time.

There was only one way to do that.

Dragging all his courage from his twisted guts, Taylor leaned over the wall and unleashed the venom of both his Colts at the braves below. It was swift, cold, calculated military precision.

It was at times like this that he thanked the Lord that he was an expert marksman. Blinding gunsmoke filled the dry air between himself and the mounted warriors. He kept firing although he was unable to see his targets. Now marksmanship took second place to sheer luck.

He heard the consequences of his actions. Whatever their origin, wounded men made the same pitiful sound whenever hot lead cut into their bodies. His bullets tore through the Cheyenne at the gates before the survivors turned their ponies and fled.

Yet the battle was not over. The rest of the attacking Indians soon replaced those who had been either wounded, killed or had just ridden away. The sound of the repeating rifles being cocked into action and fired over and over again filled Taylor's ears.

Then he was hit high in the left shoulder. The force of the Winchester bullet knocked him off his boots with the power of a mule kick. Taylor landed on his back on the very edge of the walkway. He rolled on to his side and glanced at the red sleeve bathed in sunlight.

The war cries were becoming deafening.

More of the determined braves were at the gates and testing their strength. Defying his own pain, Taylor got back to his feet. His Colts were empty and there was no time to reload either of them. Taylor holstered the hot guns, grabbed his Winchester from the parapet and leapt down into the parade ground.

With fear now overwhelming him, he started to run for the buildings on the other side of the wide expanse of sand. Every few strides he turned and fired the Winchester at the gates and walls. He knew that he could not hold them off for much longer. There were far too many of them.

He reached the officers' quarters and entered.

He turned on his heels and pushed the door shut. It refused to remain closed. Then he saw the broken lock.

'Why did I kick this damn door in?' he shouted at himself. He dragged a heavy desk across the floor until it was holding the door in its frame.

Taylor went to the window and pulled the shutters towards him. He secured them and squinted through the gap. He could see the gates clearly.

A million questions burned through his mind. Only one made any sense to him as he desperately reloaded his guns from the bullets on his belt. Blood was flowing down his arm and soaked into his shirtsleeve.

How did these Indians have so many repeating rifles? He had served in an army with less equipment than these warriors possessed. Taylor glanced at the tear in his shirtsleeve. The wound was raw and pumping blood. There was no time to tend to it though, he thought. There was only enough time to fight and die if fate decreed it.

The secret service man cocked the hammers of his handguns and inhaled deeply. His heart felt as though it had stopped for the briefest of moments when he thought of the highly painted riders he had encountered at the gates.

Then the gates burst open. Thirty or more screaming Cheyenne braves rode through the choking dust astride their ponies. The dust hung on the hot dry air. They were shooting in all directions, trying to locate their unseen enemy.

Taylor knew that his handiwork at repairing the gates was now undone but at least it had bought him the precious time he had needed to reach the officers' quarters and their sturdy walls.

The braves were riding around frantically. Taylor could see the paint on their faces and torsos in detail now. It was a sight which he would never be able to forget. A mixture of awe and fear flowed through him in equal parts.

His eyes were glued upon the ranting warriors as they fired the gleaming new weapons around the fortress. He wondered how long he had before they discovered him. Then something else drew his attention. These were not cheap rifles that they held in their hands. These were probably the most expensive Winchester models available and each of them was worth several months' wages.

So how was it that these Indians possessed them? It made no sense to his military mind. It was certain that they could never have afforded them and it would have been illegal for anyone to have sold them to hostiles anyway. So how on earth could they have such an impressive arsenal?

Chief Red Eagle swung his pony full circle as his narrowed eyes studied every structure within the high walls. It did not take the Cheyenne chief long to spot the officers' quarters and the closed window shutters.

Red Eagle pointed his rifle at the building and bellowed out at his followers. Within seconds every one of them knew where their prey was hiding. A few seconds after that they started once again to unleash their impressive firepower.

The wall made of wooden tree-trunks began to disintegrate under the ceaseless bombardment.

'Damn it all!' Taylor cursed as smouldering sawdust covered him. 'Now I'm dead for sure!'

# FIVE

No tornado could have caused such havoc. The officers' quarters' window shutters exploded inwards as scores of bullets tore into the wooden building from the rifles of the Cheyenne. To the man trapped within it seemed that every one of the mounted warriors must have opened fire at exactly the same moment. Their accuracy with the expensive repeating rifles left him in awe. The once well-carved shutters disintegrated under the relentless volleys.

Taylor was forced back from the window as choking debris smothered him. His eyes took the full impact of the burning splinters. He buckled in agony. Both his guns dropped from his hands as he vainly attempted to free his eyes from the blinding fragments.

He fell to his knees and curled up as more bullets tore through the broken window shutters.

He could hear the sound of the lethal lead as it hit the wall behind him. The smell of gunsmoke grew stronger as Taylor crawled in the opposite direction to where the gunfire was loudest.

Taylor was blinded. He prayed that it was only temporary but feared the worst. In all his days he had never known such pain before. It was as if red-hot pokers had been rammed into his eyes.

When he reached the door to the next room he felt his own rifle beneath his hands. He picked it up, rolled on to his back and cranked the Winchester into action. Taylor fired at the window as his legs continued to push him backwards. For the briefest of moments the Cheyenne were taken by surprise and halted their firing.

Then, just as the firing resumed, to his right he heard the door to the parade ground being forced by the braves. He swung the long barrel around and blasted two more shots at it. For a moment the pounding stopped.

Again it was but a brief pause in the combat.

The guttural yells of the Indians seemed to echo around him as he kept forcing himself back into the next room. At last, after what felt like an eternity, he knew that he had achieved his goal and found a place where their bullets could not reach. He placed the rifle down and clawed at the door until his hands were able to push it shut.

He dragged its bolt across and secured it.

48

Again he tried to free his eyes from the blinding splinters.

Again he failed.

He dragged himself up to his full height with his rifle across his waist. His right hand was inside the rifle guard and his index finger curled around the small cold trigger. Taylor wondered whether there were any windows in this room. His mind raced as he tried to recall what the layout of this room was. He simply could not remember.

Then he heard the sound of the Cheyenne crashing their way into the room he had just vacated. He bit his lip and felt his own tears running from his burning eyes. The pain was almost crippling but he had to keep fighting.

The alternative was to die. Taylor was not ready for that just yet.

He pushed the handguard down, then pulled it back up into position. He heard the spent shell casing as it was ejected and bounced on the boarded floor.

The door against which he was resting his back started to move violently. Shoulders and feet were hitting it with renewed venom. Taylor could hear the determined grunts and groans of the men who were trying to force their way in.

With gritted teeth he turned, pushed his Winchester barrel up against it, then squeezed the trigger. The kick knocked him backwards as his bullet blasted through the wooden door.

A muffled cry told him that he had hit one of the braves.

He knew that he had to move quickly before they retaliated with their own superior arsenal.

Blindly Taylor staggered away from the door. He felt something behind his boots but was unable to steady himself. He toppled and fell as a half-dozen shots were returned through the wooden door. Before he hit the floorboards he felt the heat of the Cheyenne's bullets as they twisted all around him. He hit the ground hard but felt no pain.

He was too desperate to feel anything except the branding-irons that still tortured his eyes. He had to return fire.

Even flat on his back Taylor swiftly cocked the rifle again and fired in the direction of the door. He wanted to keep shooting but knew that his repeating rifle had only fourteen rounds in its magazine to start with and he had already wasted at least half that number.

With his Colts gone, the Winchester was his only defence.

More bullets came bursting through the door in reply to his solitary shot. He could feel the heat of the white-hot lead as it passed over his supine frame.

Taylor rubbed his eyes again. Then one of them began to clear. It was like looking through a wall of water but at least he was able to see the door as the Cheyenne's bullets methodically destroyed it.

Fearing that they could see him, Taylor rolled over and over until he was up against a wall. Bullets tore up the floor where he had been lying a fraction of a second earlier. He managed to get up on to one knee and push the handguard down and back up again. Another of his precious bullets was now ready to be fired.

Taylor watched as the centre of the door came crashing inwards. Rifle barrels pounded the already weakened wood before even more bullets entered the room.

Without hesitation the kneeling man fired.

Taylor's shot passed straight through the break. There was a cry followed by a thud from beyond the door. Taylor knew that he had hit one of the Indians but there were still far too many of them to kill with his ever reducing supply of bullets.

He gritted his teeth and sent another bullet through the hole in the door. Again he knew that he had hit one of the warriors but they refused to stop either their shooting or their assault on the door.

The pounding seemed to be becoming even more intense. The door was starting to buckle and shatter with every fistbeat. The hole became even bigger.

Even with only one eye capable of seeing properly, Taylor saw the braves illuminated in the sunlight which came from the parade ground behind them.

He inhaled. There was nothing left to do but go down fighting. However few bullets he had remaining in the magazine of the Winchester he had to use them all now, he silently told himself.

Again Taylor quickly pushed the rifle guard down, dragged it back up and fired. He kept repeating his deadly action and watched as brave after brave fell backwards.

To his horror they kept on coming to the door. They knew that the trapped man would run out of ammunition before they did.

They were right.

It had taken less than a minute. Taylor's finger felt the trigger action of the rifle slacken. The Winchester was empty. He rose to his feet and turned the rifle around until he was holding its long, hot barrel. He rested his back against the wooden wall and waited for the gunsmoke to clear.

Now he would use the rifle as a club if he had a chance. The tall man knew that it was doubtful that once the Cheyenne braves entered the room he would live long enough to swing it. They would more than likely cut him down with bullets in revenge for those he had been forced to slay.

Taylor resolved to die like a man. Whether it be a quick or a slow death, he would take it standing up for as long as he were able.

Suddenly as the door began to break away from its hinges he heard another sound from outside. A sound which even rose above the war chants and the bullet-firing.

His heart quickened.

It was a bugle.

A bugler was sounding 'Charge!'

# SIX

There was no music more terrifying to those who recognized its grim warning than that of a solitary army bugler playing 'Charge'. It could turn even the stoutest of men into fearful cowards. If they had also witnessed and tasted the cavalry sabres' wrath, they would never forget it if they lived to be a hundred years old.

The Cheyenne had fallen prey to many such encounters before they had been forcibly evicted from their ancestral hunting-grounds and moved to this desolate and worthless land; a land they shared not only with its native Apaches but with other broken tribes.

Chief Red Eagle and his braves recognized the tune being blown through the distant bugle. They had all heard it before, before being charged by cavalrymen. Cavalrymen were soldiers who had been trained to kill all who stood in their way. The chief started to give his men frantic orders. They

54

all turned away from the broken door and ran out of the building to their waiting ponies.

The braves picked up their wounded and thundered off towards the high ridge. Red Eagle knew that their numbers had been whittled down too far for them to contemplate engaging well-trained cavalrymen.

Even after they had fled Taylor was still shaking in a mixture of fear and total bewilderment. This had been his first encounter with Indians and he prayed it would be his last.

He could not believe his good fortune. Somehow he was still alive. Taylor staggered to the door and pulled what was left of it off its hinges. He stepped over the dead Indians and made his way to his pair of Colts. They were still where he had dropped them only minutes earlier. Taylor studied the floor with a military eye. He soon realized that any wounded Indians had been taken from the scene. The trails of blood marking the floorboards were evidence of that.

The bugle was still ringing out in the hot afternoon air as Taylor scooped up his Colts and holstered them. He ventured out on to the parade ground with the rifle under his arm, then paused for a moment to ensure that his attackers were finally gone.

He could hear the Cheyenne ponies thundering away.

The exhausted man felt the wound on his upper arm as at last it began to hurt. He glanced at it and wondered why he had not felt any pain when he was fighting for his very survival. It was only a graze but it had bled like fury. Taylor walked to one of the troughs and looked at the water. He rested the rifle against the trough, leaned forward, then lowered his face into the cooling water.

He raised himself back up and relished the water as it drenched over him. He blinked hard and eventually began to see with both his eyes. Taylor pushed his face back into the water and shook his head.

Then, even with his head under the water, he realized that something had changed. Something was definitely different. Taylor emerged from the trough once more and stared out through the gap where the gates had been before the Cheyenne had decided to batter them into matchwood.

The dust still hung on the afternoon air showing that the Indians had retreated to where they had come from, beyond the ridge. Scott Taylor did not know it but by diverting their attention for a few brief minutes he had managed to save the lives of the settlers down on Blood River.

Taylor patted the palm of his right hand against his ear and turned his head. The silence screamed at his senses. He was suddenly aware that the bugle had stopped playing its blood-curdling tune as suddenly as it had started.

He wondered why.

His eyes darted back to the dust. The Cheyenne had gone, he told himself. But for how long?

The tall man knew that the sound of the bugle had saved his hide but wondered why it had stopped. He also wondered what a cavalry troop was doing in this neck of the desert. To the best of his knowledge there had been no cavalrymen in these parts for years, at the time when Fort Briggs was fully manned.

Instinctively, Taylor plucked bullets from his gunbelt and began to reload his handguns as fast as he had ever done before.

When he had completed his task he lifted the rifle and walked to the gates. He was surprised by the number of dead Indians there were littering the blood-soaked sand. A few of their ponies wandered aimlessly around as if waiting for their dead masters to come miraculously back to life.

Taylor looked at his handiwork. So many bodies. He counted seven. He felt no satisfaction, only sadness. Killing had become part of his life and he took no pleasure in it.

He sighed. It was a sigh of shame.

Suddenly the bugle sounded again. It startled him. Taylor spun on his heels and looked to where the sound was coming from. A sandy rise stood more than twenty feet high a quarter of a mile away to the west of the fortress. He could hear the bugle getting louder.

Patiently he waited.

The sight that greeted his sore eyes was not what he had expected. Taylor blinked hard.

His eyes were not lying to him.

# SEVEN

Colonel Joshua Morgan fitted his description to the letter. Yet the broad smile that filled his aging features came as a shock to the bloodied Taylor. The lone rider who led a heavily laden packhorse sat like the Union officer he had once been. Yet his clothing bore little or no suggestion of his previous career. He wore a suit of heavy dark material. He also wore a topcoat more suited to northern climates than to the heat here in the middle of an arid landscape. The thing that Taylor noticed most of all was the bugle in Morgan's left hand, resting on his thigh.

So this was the troop of cavalry that he and the Cheyenne had expected, Taylor thought. As the rider got closer Taylor spied a large ball of tumble-weed tied to the tail of the packhorse. It made a lot of dust rise, just as it was intended to do.

Taylor shook his head as the horseman drew up beside him.

'Morgan?' Taylor enquired.

'Damn right, pally!' Morgan smiled. 'You look kinda disappointed. Are you disappointed?'

Taylor sighed. 'In a way I am. I was hoping there'd be a few dozen troopers headed here just in case them Indians come back for seconds.'

Morgan looked to where the pony tracks were and then back at Taylor.

'They'll be back OK, Taylor. Not for a while, though.'

Thoughtfully, Taylor followed the horse as its master steered his mount through the open gateway into the parade ground and the welcoming troughs.

'You seem to know a lot about them, Morgan.'

'I do.' Morgan agreed cheerfully. 'Their main camp is about fifteen miles south of here. They're taking their injured back there so their women and medicine man can tend their wounds. By the time they reach the camp it'll be dark. They won't come back here until sun-up. Reckon we got until tomorrow afternoon before we sets eyes on them again. By which time I for one intend to be some-place else.'

'Thank God!' Taylor said loudly. 'I sure ain't up to another tussle with them today and that's for certain!'

'You sure landed yourself in a whole heap of trouble here, pally.' Morgan reined in and dismounted. He allowed both his animals to drink from the closest trough before cutting the tumbleweed from the tail of his packhorse. 'I was here just after dawn myself. I seen the smoke start and reckoned it was smart to head on out.'

Taylor rested his hands on the wall of the well. 'I sure could have used your help when they attacked me.'

Morgan smiled. 'I filled the troughs for you.'

'I mean with the fighting, Morgan.' Taylor turned his head and studied the curious figure. 'I could have been killed here and I ain't sure how I wasn't.'

The older man sat down on the edge of the trough and stared at the exhausted Taylor. He gave a knowing nod.

'You handled yourself pretty well on your own by the looks of those dead 'uns scattered out there.'

'It would have been nice to have had help with that, though.'

'That ain't why I'm here, pally.' Morgan pulled out a pipe and placed its stem between his teeth. 'I'm here to give you your sealed orders, not get mixed up in no Indian war.'

Taylor held out a hand. 'Go on then. Give them to me like you're supposed to do! I figure someone already knows what's in them, though.'

Morgan frowned. 'It'd sure seem that way.'

'I was attacked out there on the way from Adobe Wells.' Taylor gestured. 'Someone knew I was coming here.'

'Kid Dynamite!' Morgan said the name as though it were poisonous.

Taylor screwed up his eyes and focused hard. 'How'd you know it was the Kid who tried to bushwhack me, Morgan?'

'I ain't deaf, pally.' Morgan retorted. 'I heard them sticks of dynamite going off.'

'Oh!' Taylor shrugged.

Morgan reached into his inside jacket pocket. He pulled out an envelope. It was sealed. He gave it to Taylor and than watched as it was opened.

'I got me a thought, pally.'

Taylor looked up from the paper at the wise face. 'Yeah? What kinda thought would that be, Morgan?'

'You might not be able to keep following those orders. They were all written down before you got on the train here. The trouble with them is that the writer didn't know that you've been sold out, pally. I got me an idea that if you do follow them orders to the letter you'll be planted in boot hill before you can spit! The last couple of folks sent down here tried to stick to the book and that's where they ended up.'

'Spill it!' Taylor stared hard at Morgan. 'How do

you know so much?'

'Simple! I've been stuck in San Remas for the best part of two years watching and listening. I've learned a lot and sent every scrap of information I've gathered back East. I just know that those orders you're holding are a tad tainted.' Morgan shrugged. 'The last couple of secret service boys who were sent down here were betrayed. I've only survived being killed because I use a fake handle. Carter and his gunslingers know about Josh Morgan but they don't know about Pop Parker. That's what I call myself in town, pally. Pop Parker, proprietor of the general store.'

'I suspected as much but it sure gnaws at your craw knowing you're right.' Taylor snorted through his flared nostrils. He was angry. Real angry.

'Cody Carter's smart. He knows that you're headed to San Remas.' Morgan offered. 'I know because I live in San Remas and folks talk. Carter bought some bastard back East. His dirty money has managed to find the pocketbook of one of the top secret service men back there. I'd give my right arm to know the name of that filthy traitor.'

Taylor returned his eyes to the paper in his hands and sighed heavily. He crumpled it up.

'Then my mission is over.' he said. 'I might as well head back if they're expecting me.'

'Hold your horses, pally!' Morgan raised a white

eyebrow and pointed at the dead Indians strewn outside the gates. 'I've got me a feeling that we might be able to use this carnage to our advantage.'

Taylor was curious. 'How?'

Morgan struck a match, held its flame above the pipe-bowl and sucked a few times. Smoke billowed from his mouth. His eyes were staring away from his companion as his quicksilver mind constructed a plan.

'Carter knows that Scott Taylor is headed to town.'

'And?'

'Then you have to become someone else.' Morgan puffed on the pipe-stem. 'You gotta fool him and his hired vermin.'

'Like who?'

'Like someone who's the complete opposite of Scott Taylor.' Morgan suggested. 'Pop Parker's nephew Ethan Parker. How does that sound?'

Taylor had had experience of taking on other personas but until now had not thought it would be necessary in this case. He rubbed his neck.

'You reckon they'd swallow that? They're expecting me to show up and suddenly another man shows up. How dumb are they?'

Morgan pointed his pipe at Taylor. 'They wouldn't swallow it if you just rode in. We have to create an illusion. We have to make them believe Scott

Taylor is dead first.'

'But how do we do that? We'd need the body of a white man. I don't see and dead white folks around here.'

'Not really, pally,' Morgan argued as pipesmoke drifted from his mouth. 'Any body will do if we dress it up right.'

'I'm starting get your drift, Morgan,' Taylor said. 'But the detail is still kinda foggy.'

The older man rose to his feet. A smile etched his wrinkled features. 'If they think that Scott Taylor was killed by the Cheyenne they won't question Ethan Parker's being genuine.'

'How do we achieve that?' Taylor narrowed his eyes and looked hard at the man beside him. He knew that Morgan had a reputation for being one of the best agents the secret service had. 'We need a body and the only ones around here are Indians and they ain't white. You figuring on whitewashing one of them poor critters?'

Morgan waved his left hand in the direction of the gates.

'Take your pick, pally! Any one of them will do.'

'But none of them looks like a white man.' Taylor repeated his fears.

Morgan puffed the last of the smoke from his pipe and then removed it from his lips. 'Ever seen a white man staked out by Indians, pally?'

'Nope.'

'I've seen plenty in my days out here. I've seen white folks tortured and killed in a whole bunch of ways.' Morgan added. 'All it'll take is a change of clothes. A slight trimming of the hair on one of them bucks and a good old-fashioned fire.'

'A fire?' Taylor stepped back in shock.

Morgan nodded. 'Yep. A well-handled fire. Believe me, when I'm finished with that dead Indian, Cody Carter and his cohorts will believe Scott Taylor's not only dead but his soul is roasting in Hell itself!'

Taylor swallowed hard. 'You're gonna set fire to one of them bodies?'

'Not until you change clothes with it, pally. Strip off them rags!' Morgan said calmly as he patted the packhorse's heavy burden. 'We need to dress up one of them bodies in your clothes and stuff his pockets with any identification papers you might have. Under this blanket I've got me a full outfit that'll fit you like a glove. Once we got your pants and shirt on that Cheyenne we'll take him to just outside the officers' quarters.'

Taylor ripped what was left of his shirt from his lean torso and dropped it to the ground. He then lifted the blanket from the back of the horse and saw the shirt and pants beside a pair of boots. His eyes flashed to Morgan as he pulled the garments free.

'You know my size?'

'Sure do!'

'You're starting to trouble me, Morgan.'

Morgan smiled. 'That's good! You might just live a little while longer.'

The packhorse had been stripped down until Taylor was able to mount it. His long legs dangled to either side of its bare back. He sat holding the reins and watched as Morgan tirelessly finished his handiwork. The older man had expertly set the wooden buildings alight. Black smoke curled up into the late afternoon sky as the dry, weathered structure was engulfed by the ravenous flames until only red embers remained amid the fragmenting blackened framework.

With no sign of emotion Josh Morgan completed his gruesome task by pouring kerosene over the head and hands of the prostrate corpse. This fire was controlled and deliberate. Only the head and hands of the Cheyenne warrior's body were burned until the man was impossible to recognize.

Satisfied, Morgan walked to his waiting mount. He looked up at Taylor, who had been watching his every action.

'It had to be done this way, pally,' Morgan bluntly announced before mounting his horse.

Taylor looked away from Morgan. He stared silently at the body. Flames rose from its head and hands but as it was wearing his clothes and even his gunbelt with its matched pair of Colts in the holsters it appeared to be him.

It was like looking at his own dead body. A cold shudder traced his spine. His eyes lifted to the rider beside him.

'I feel kinda naked without my guns.'

'I'll give you guns when we get back to my store,' Morgan said coldly. He pulled his reins and turned his horse.

'Why do I have to leave my saddle here?' Taylor questioned. 'Bad enough leaving my mount.'

Morgan glanced at Taylor. 'We have to make this look real. If the Cheyenne had killed you they'd not want your saddle, so that's why we left it in the stables. I set the horse loose so it would look as if the critter had spooked and run off before the Indians could get their hands on it. Besides, if I'd ridden to Adobe Wells to pick up my nephew from the train depot it's doubtful he'd have either a horse or a saddle with him. right?'

Taylor nodded. 'I guess so.'

'This has gotta look real, pally. Cody Carter and his men ain't stupid. You have to become my nephew. If you believe it then we have a chance that they will as well. Otherwise we'll both get ourselves killed pretty damn quick.'

Taylor adjusted himself on the back of the pack-horse. 'I sure miss that padded saddle, though.'

Morgan tapped his spurs against the sides of his horse and started to ride. Taylor kept pace with the older horseman even though he had never ridden bareback before.

Long after the sun had disappeared below the distant horizon an eerie scarlet glow pulsated like a beating heart above the fort.

The two riders headed west towards San Remas.

# EIGHT

The small town of San Remas was just like every other settlement in the territory when night fell. As soon as the street lanterns were lit and their amber light fell from the high poles upon which they were perched the sandy streets somehow came to life. Not the same life as existed during the hours of daylight but a totally different life. This was when the respectable people disappeared from view and the human vermin cascaded out of their ratholes to drink and womanize their nights away. The cantinas, brothels and saloons did a roaring trade thanks, in the main, to their ruthless benefactor Cody Carter. His money flowed from one place to another like rivers of corruption.

His money had soiled the once peaceful town until it was barely recognizable to anyone who had ever visited it before Carter had arrived with his army of henchmen. The few establishments which did not have his name brandished upon their façades were tolerated by Carter. He knew that even he had to have a little competition if he were to be able to steal others' hard-earned cash.

The lanterns stretched down every street and alley. They sent their light pouring upon those who ventured down the town's boardwalks. Every saloon was full to overflowing but the Carter Cartwheel was where the most villainous of all spent their nights and money. A tinny piano was being played in the corner of the saloon by a man who relied upon free beer to fuel his stamina as Carter's small legion of killers drank yet another evening away.

Carter's top gun, Jackson Wright, rested one elbow on the bar counter and stared into the thin glass that he held in his right hand. It was empty, he had run out of money and he still had a thirst. The large man surveyed all that lay around him with a knowing eye. Twelve of Carter's other men were in various parts of the large saloon, in varying stages of drunkenness.

Wright straightened up and tripped over the spittoon at his feet before making his way towards the closest table, where three of his fellow hired guns sat watching an almost empty whiskey bottle in the centre of the green baize.

'You boys oughta go back to the hotel and get some shuteye!' Wright blasted as he reached the trio.

71

Brad Green, George Hume and Pete Smith were not drunk enough to swallow that. They knew that Carter's number one gun was on the prowl for free liquor.

Green reached across the table and snatched at the bottle. He held it close to his chest and looked up into the fiery face of Wright.

'Beat it, Jack!' Green snarled.

Wright rested his hands on the back of Smith's chair and glared from beneath his hat brim at the man nursing the bottle.

'You say something, Brad?'

'Buy ya own whiskey, Jackson!' Hume said. He lifted his full glass and swallowed its contents in one toss. 'Carter pays you more than the rest of us. It ain't our fault your thirst is bigger than ya wallet.'

Wright gripped the chair-back hard. His knuckles went white as he inhaled deeply. Since they had hired on, none of the three men had ever seen Wright show his true colours. None of them knew whether he was worth the extra money Carter paid him. One of them had a desire to find out.

'I ain't afraid of you, Jack,' Green announced in a tone that could do nothing but make Wright even angrier than he already was.

Wright glared at Green. 'I'm the ramrod of this outfit and what I say goes. Get going!'

Green filled his own glass and handed the bottle

to Hume.

'George's right, Jack. You got enough money to buy ya own liquor. So go do it!'

'That's fighting talk, ya li'l bastard!' Wright released his grip on the chair and straighted up. Smith could feel the hot breath on his neck and moved chairs as fast as his drunken legs could manage. 'I've killed men for less!'

Green pushed his hat back off his face. He stared up at Wright, whose hands were now hovering above his gun grips. Green showed no fear.

'When I joined this outfit I thought we were gonna do something harder than selling rifles and whiskey to Indians, Jack.' Green sank his whiskey and placed the empty glass down on the table. 'All we seem to do is protect that overweight Carter from getting his butt shot up. You might cotton to that but I don't.'

'Me neither,' Smith agreed.

Wright was furious. His yellow broken teeth started to show between his unshaven lips.

'I'm gonna kill you, Brad!' he vowed.

'Do it if ya can!' Green flexed his fingers and drew his arm back until it was above the handle of his holstered Remington .45. Still seated, the man showed no fear. 'I ain't afraid of a drunk.'

Hume cleared his throat and raised the bottle. 'Easy, Brad! There's enough whiskey in here for him to have a glass.'

'No, there ain't!' Green contradicted.

The saloon suddenly went quiet. The piano stopped playing and the rest of the gunfighters seated around the room stared in the direction of the table where Wright and the three hired guns were. A fight was brewing and they all knew it.

'You gonna let me have that whiskey or are ya just gonna die, Brad?' Wright snorted. 'Which'll it be?'

'You know the answer to that one, Jack!' Green's hand was a mere inch above his holstered gun. 'Go on and scare me if you can!'

'I don't want none of this.' Smith pushed his chair away from the table and got to his feet. He staggered away towards the rest of Carter's hired men now gathered close to the bar counter. 'They're loco!'

'Pete's right! This is plumb loco!' Hume licked his lips and placed the bottle back on the table. 'Have it, Jackson! I'll buy us another bottle. Go on! Take it!'

A wry smile etched Wright's face. 'Ya pal's got sense, Brad. You ready to stand down?'

Green said nothing.

'I asked you a question, little man,' Wright sneered loudly.

Green tilted his head. 'OK! Take it, Jack! You need it more than I do.'

Wright gave a short chuckle. Victory was a hard

thing for someone like Wright to hide. He leaned across the chair and table and plucked the bottle off the green baize. His blurred eyes focused upon the mere two inches of whiskey inside the clear glass.

'Next time, don't try and stand up to a real man, Brad!'

The words had barely left his smiling lips when the sound of metal leaving leather filled the ears of everyone in the saloon. A deafening shot followed within a split second and echoed all around the large room. Gunsmoke rose from the edge of the table as Jackson Wright's expression suddenly changed in full realization of what had just occurred.

His smile disappeared. The bottle slid from his fingers and hit the table. Miraculously it remained upright. Jackson blinked, then looked down at his waist. The hole was big and brutal.

It went clean through him.

Green spun the .45 on his trigger finger and blew down its smoking barrel. As he watched Wright fall like a felled tree he started to smile. He stood and picked up the bottle and walked to where Wright lay open-eyed on the bloody sawdust. The body was shaking as life slowly evaporated from its frame.

'Reckon you might as well have the whiskey, Jack!' Green smirked and poured the last of the bottle's contents over the twisted face. 'You need it more than me where you're going!'

The swing doors of the saloon opened and Kid Dynamite stood with a hand on them. He looked down at the man on the floor and then back at Green.

'That deserves a drink, Brad,' the Kid said. 'You done pretty good killing that rat. Saved me a job!'

'Carter ain't gonna like this,' Hume told anyone willing to listen to him. No one was. The crowd started to gather around Green as he tossed the empty bottle away.

Kid Dynamite strode into the saloon. He tossed a golden coin at the bartender.

'The drinks are on me! I feel kinda happy!'

# NINE

The solitary gunshot echoed all around the border town like a clap of thunder. Its chilling noise alerted both of the riders to the danger to which they were exposing themselves simply by entering the boundaries of San Remas. The secret service men knew that their superiors back East might have been correct in deeming this a suicide mission. The odds were stacked against them higher than anything else they had ever tackled.

Josh Morgan reined in and gave his companion a quick glance which spoke louder than words. He said nothing as the packhorse drew alongside his own dust-caked animal and also stopped.

Taylor rubbed the dust from his face and gave a long hard stare at the array of buildings which faced them. San Remas's lights sparkled in the evening desert air like jewels in a priceless necklace. Its beauty belied the dangers which lurked unchecked within the small border settlement.

'The town's still wide awake by the sounds of it, Morgan,' Taylor said.

'Pop!' corrected Morgan sternly. 'I'm Pop! Never call me by my real name or you'll be signing my death sentence!'

Taylor was weary but knew that that was no excuse. 'Sorry, Pop! I guess I'm still a bit punch drunk from my meeting with them Cheyenne.'

Morgan leaned across the distance between them. 'I hope you realize that if they kill me they'll certainly kill you as well, pally.'

Taylor nodded. 'I'm tuckered but I ain't dumb.'

'Good enough.' Morgan returned his attention to the brightly illuminated town in front of them. 'I sure hope we can figure out who the traitor back East is. If we only discover that, we'll at least stop some of the carnage that'll surely follow us here.'

'Carter must have the name of the traitor written down somewhere, Pop,' Taylor said. 'Reckon he don't think anyone might try and find that name.'

Morgan nodded. 'Right enough.'

Taylor looked at the older man again. 'Say, have you wondered why them Cheyenne were so ornery? I thought that they were peace-loving! And another thing, how come they had so many brand-new Winchesters?'

'The answer to your questions is simple,

Ethan,' Morgan replied trying to get used to the fabricated name he had chosen for his ally. 'Cody Carter.'

The younger horseman looked at his fellow rider. 'How can a white man get an entire tribe so angry?'

'A mixture of whiskey and weapons, pally,' Morgan said bluntly. 'That lowlife has been supplying them with plenty of both so that they'll do his dirty work for him. I've suspected as much for a long time but knowing and proving are two mighty different things.'

'Those Indians were drunk?'

'Didn't you smell the liquor on them?'

'I tried not to let them get that close.'

Morgan grinned. 'I smelled it on the one I roasted. Man, that was a powerful brew! I reckon I could have set fire to his breath without the kerosene.'

Scott Taylor thought about those he had yet to meet in the town in front of them. Men who killed because they were paid to kill and had no other reason apart from their actually liking it. He still felt vulnerable without any weaponry but would not reveal his anxiety to Morgan. Taylor knew that the seasoned campaigner required strength from him, not doubts.

'C'mon, Ethan!' Josh Morgan gathered up his reins and tapped his spurs against the sides of his mount. 'I figure the first thing we have to do is give Carter a visit.'

Taylor urged his horse on. 'We do what?'

'Don't go fretting none, Ethan!' Morgan said over his shoulder. 'I got it all worked out. We have to confront him and let him know about the trouble at Fort Briggs. Carter has to go there with his men and find that body. He also has to meet you, my dearest nephew.'

Taylor drew his horse level with Morgan's. 'Poor Scott Taylor! He didn't stand a chance against all those Cheyenne!'

'Now you're starting to get it, pally.'

The two horsemen rode through the darkness until the torch- and lantern-light of Carter's impressive home cascaded over them in all its glory. Both riders stopped their horses outside the large house. Neither man dismounted until they saw the figure of Cody Carter looking down upon them from the high balcony. Morgan touched the brim of his hat, eased himself off his horse and brushed the trail grime from his heavy clothing. He handed his reins to his companion and stepped into the light of a blazing wall torch.

'Mr Carter,' Morgan acknowledged.

'What you want here, Pop?' Carter asked from his lofty perch. 'Don't tell me that my boys have been shooting up your store again!'

'Nope. Nothing like that. Me and my nephew

here found a whole heap of bodies out at Fort Briggs a few hours back, Mr Carter,' Morgan replied. 'One of the critters was a white varmint! I was wondering if you might have lost one of your men.'

Carter rested his hands upon the balcony rail and looked down hard at the general store owner.

'You sure about that, Pop?'

'Yep,' Morgan nodded. 'We seen a big cloud of smoke and went to investigate. Half the fort has been torched. Looks like there was a ruckus there. A lot of Indians killed, but they must have got the white varmint who was dumb enough to stand up against them! His body was staked out and set alight! Are you missing anyone?'

'All my boys are accounted for, Pop.'

'Then who on earth was that critter?' Morgan looked down and continued his deception. 'Who could he have been, I wonder?'

'Taylor,' Carter said quietly to himself.

'I figured you'd want to know,' Morgan said.

'You were right, Pop,' Carter replied. A triumphant smile crossed his face. 'This is my county and I want to know everything that's happened within its confines.'

Morgan touched his hat brim, turned and accepted his reins back from Taylor. He was about to step into his stirrup when the words he had known would come eventually arrived.

'Who is that with you, Pop?'

Morgan pulled himself back on top of his saddle and looked up at the face he secretly loathed. 'Why, this is my nephew Ethan, Mr Carter. Ethan Parker. My brother's boy. I had to ride to Adobe Wells to pick him up off the train.'

Carter curled a finger at Taylor. 'Move into the light, Ethan. I want to get me a good look at you, son.'

Taylor obeyed and allowed his mount to take two steps forward. He saw the light spread over his hands as they rested upon the saddle horn. It crept up his chest until he was forced to half-close his eyes against its brightness. He looked up and smiled.

'Howdy, sir.'

Carter nodded. 'You staying with your uncle long?'

Again Taylor nodded. 'Sure am, sir. Pop's gonna teach me the business so I can be a businessman just like him one day.'

Thoughtfully, Carter rubbed his chin and turned his eyes back on Morgan.

'Could you go to the Cartwheel and tell my boys that I want them, Pop? I want them here now.'

'My pleasure, Mr Carter.' Morgan touched the brim of his Stetson again and turned the head of his horse away from the large house. He gave Taylor a knowing nod and whispered out of the corner of his mouth: 'C'mon, pally. We're done here.'

Cody Carter watched the pair of horsemen ride away under the lights of the long dark street towards the saloon. He knew something was wrong but could not work out exactly what.

The old colonel's bluff had been better than any riverboat gambler with five useless cards in his hand.

'You can start breathing again, pally,' Morgan said out of the corner of his mouth.

Taylor swallowed. 'You sure got some nerve, Uncle.'

Cody Carter turned, walked back into his house and waited.

# TEN

It was a relieved Scott Taylor who followed the older man into the rear of the store and bolted its sturdy rear door behind them both. He recalled the spoken orders he had been given back East by one of the four top secret service officers. His main duty in accepting the mission to the Arizona territory was to try to discover any evidence of the many crimes known to have been committed by Carter and his gang. If he could manage that he had to attempt either to arrest the man or go one step further and kill him. The law did not have the same meaning in the territories as they had in fully fledged states. Yet the government was committed to try to protect those who were attempting to settle even the most barren parts of America.

It was a tall, if not an impossible, order.

The lamps lit by Morgan on his way to the makeshift parlour lured the younger man. Taylor trailed Morgan through the stockroom and stopped when he saw the easy chairs, small table and the stove. Morgan opened the blackened stove door and added a few logs to its glowing embers.

'Coffee, pally?'

Taylor nodded and seated himself at the kitchen table. 'You got a nice place here, pop.'

Morgan chuckled. 'This ain't mine,' he corrected. 'This belongs to our dear old uncle Sam. It's just a base for us to use until the next assignment.'

Taylor nodded. 'What about those guns you promised me? I'm still feeling kinda naked without them.'

Morgan checked the coffee pot and placed it on top of the stove. He then walked to a large wooden chest beside the doorway to the store itself, leaned over and lifted its lid. He glanced across at Taylor.

'You favour Colt .45s?'

'Yep,' Taylor nodded again.

Morgan's hands searched and then found two handsome weapons and an equally handsome, well-stitched gunbelt. He straightened up and held the weapons out to his fellow agent.

'Will these do?'

Taylor rose and walked over to Morgan. He accepted the guns and belt and studied them with an expert eye.

'Brand-new?'

Morgan nodded. 'Yep. Straight from Sam Colt's factory. There's plenty of ammo in the store.'

Taylor looped the belt around his waist and did up its buckle. He adjusted it and then dropped both the guns into the holsters. A few fast draws later he relaxed into a smile.

'Almost as good as my old shooting rig.'

'Better.' Morgan dropped the lid and walked back to the stove where he found two clean tin cups.

After Taylor had found a box of .45 bullets in the store he returned to the kitchen. He started to load the guns and then filled the bullet loops on his belt with as many shells as they could handle.

'I wonder if we can find something to bring Carter to book, Uncle?' he drawled. 'Unless he does something directly to us our hands are tied. We need proof.'

Morgan touched the side of the pot with the back of his left hand and looked at Taylor.

'That's gonna be the toughest thing. I've been here for two years and not been able to pin anything on him. Carter somehow manages to be as slippery as an eel.'

'And we can't take the law into our own hands without sinking to his level,' Taylor sighed.

'He has to make a mistake sometime though.' Morgan gave a shrug. 'I just hope I don't die of old age before that happens.'

'Is there a bank in town?'

'Yep,' Morgan replied. 'Guess who owns it.'

Taylor bit his lip. 'Have you tried to break in there and see if there are documents or the like which might condemn him?'

Morgan shook his head. 'Nope. I figured that would be just plumb loco. Why get shot as a bank robber?'

Both men fell silent for a while. Then Taylor looked at his colleague and grinned.

'I have to admit it, Pop,' Taylor stated. 'I never seen or heard anyone spill so many lies so damn convincingly as you did to Carter.'

'Takes a lot of practice to lie that honestly, pally.'

'Reckon so.'

A contented Cody Carter was standing inside one of his most luxurious rooms when the fourteen gunslingers tramped up the stairs and entered noisily. Until that moment all he had thought about was the image of yet another secret service man lying face down in his own blood. His expression and mood altered when he realized how quiet his men were. Each of them moved to a separate chair and seated himself. Only when they had rested their bones did the ruthless Carter notice that one of them was missing.

'Where's Jack?' He asked them as his eyes went from one to another. Only when they reached

Hume did he spot a nervousness he had not noticed before. Carter walked to the troubled figure and pushed him back on his chair. 'I asked you a damn question and I reckon you better answer me, George! Where the hell is Jack?'

Before Hume could open his mouth Brad Green rose to his feet and walked arrogantly towards his paymaster.

'I killed him, Carter!' Green boasted. 'I killed your top gun and I'd do it again given a chance.'

Carter turned and faced the small, thin man. His glare alone stopped Green in his tracks.

'You did what?' Carter growled.

'I killed him!' Green repeated. 'One shot and the fat bastard just folded up and died. Shame you missed it.'

Cody Carter drew a deep breath, lowered his head and walked across the room to a table topped with decanters filled to their crystal stoppers with expensive liquors. He removed one of the stoppers, lifted the decanter and poured a large measure into a brandy glass. He took a large swallow and then placed the glass down. Again he took a long inhalation of air before facing his men.

'Why?' Carter asked Green as every one of the seated men watched the pair square up to one another. 'Why would you do that, Brad?'

'I felt like it!' Green snapped back. 'I figured it was time you had a new number one boy, Carter.

Jack was slow and that don't cut the mustard in our profession.'

Carter nodded and then started to walk to the balcony. As he passed Green he indicated for the gunfighter to follow. Green did.

'Where you going, boss?' Kid Dynamite asked.

Carter patted the Kid's shoulder. 'Stay here! I'll be speaking to you next, Kid.'

Brad Green was laughing as he trailed Carter out into the fresh air. He rested a hip on the balcony rail and gave the town a glance.

'Well?' Green asked. 'I'm listening.'

Carter had been a renowned gunfighter in his earlier days. Long before he had the money to surround himself with hired guns the now overweight man had known what it felt like to be the fastest draw. In all his days he had never met anyone who could come close to the speed that he had once possessed.

Was he still as fast? Carter silently asked himself

'I asked you a question, Carter.' Green raised his voice.

'I heard you.' Cody Carter exhaled, then reached inside his frock-coat. Faster than Green had ever seen a hand move he watched as if frozen to the spot as his eyes saw the gun appearing. A thumb cocked its hammer as a finger squeezed its trigger.

The gun blasted. It lit up the darkness. The

white flash tore from the barrel and hit the gunfighter dead centre. The sheer impact knocked Green over the rail. There was no sound until the body hit the ground below the balcony. Carter leaned over the rail and looked briefly at the corpse with the gaping hole in its chest.

With smoke trailing from the barrel of the gun in his hand, Carter walked back into the room and looked at the faces of the thirteen stunned men. He raised the weapon and pointed at the Kid.

Kid Dynamite gasped. 'I ain't done nothing, boss!'

'I know that, Kid. You're now my top gun. Get our horses ready because we got a long ride ahead of us!'

The Kid stood. 'Where we going?'

'Fort Briggs.' Carter pushed the gun back into its hidden holster and rubbed his hands together.

'Why there?'

'Pop Parker told me he's seen a dead white man there!' Carter answered. 'I want to find out if he was telling the truth.'

'Could it have been that *hombre* I tried to blow up?' The Kid started to rouse a few of the others to their feet to help him get their horses from the stables.

Carter smiled. 'I sure hope so, Kid!'

Pete Smith reluctantly rose from his chair and cleared his throat. He was terrified. For the first time he had seen how dangerous his employer truly was.

'Mr Carter? Can I ask why you done that to Brad? I know he killed Wright but—'

'Why did I kill Brad?' Carter repeated the question out loud. 'Because I can, Pete! Just because I can! Besides, his sort are trouble. You can't turn your back on them without tempting a bullet.'

There were no more questions. Kid Dynamite led the dozen others out of the room and down the carpeted staircase. Cody Carter strolled behind them.

Now his thoughts drifted back to Fort Briggs and the reported charred human remains Parker had claimed to have discovered. Had his well-supplied Cheyenne warriors managed to do what the Kid had failed to achieve?

Carter had to find out for himself. This was no job to be given to underlings.

The night air was bracing as he walked out to the waiting horses and the men who now showed him total respect. Carter mounted and swung his white gelding around. He spurred and led them out of San Remas at a blistering pace.

# ELEVEN

The entire wooden structure of the general store shook as though a small tornado had just passed across it. The sound of hoofs had filled the building as the fourteen horseman drove their charges along the main thoroughfare and out into the desert. Taylor and Morgan looked at one another over the table.

'Did you hear that?' Taylor asked his companion. Before Morgan could respond Taylor had left his supper, marched through the dark hardware store and pressed himself up against the glass of its front door. He stared out into the lantern light at the dust which still eddied along the entire length of the wide street.

'What you so all fired up about, pally?' Morgan asked as he caught up with Taylor.

'Horses,' Taylor answered. 'A whole bunch of them.'

'Probably just local boys heading back to their—'

'No!' Taylor said firmly. 'It wasn't just cowboys. It was Carter's men.'

Morgan placed a hand on Taylor's shoulder and turned the younger man.

'How can you be so sure?'

'Look!' Taylor raised a hand and aimed a finger. The dust was still hanging along the length of the street. It originated outside the huge mansion that Cody Carter called his home. 'It was his men. Carter must have sent them to the old fort to check out your story.'

'It don't mean that all his men rode out.'

Taylor gave a smile. 'Maybe not but I figure that Carter was with them.'

Again Morgan frowned. 'How can you be so sure?'

'Because you spun a mighty fine hook back there and I reckon Carter swallowed it.' Taylor rubbed his neck anxiously 'This could be our chance to search his house. Our chance to see if we can find some evidence that'll hang that crook. If they have all ridden out this could be our only chance.'

'Hold on there, pally!' Morgan could see the spirit he once possessed in equal measure burning in the eyes of Taylor. 'I can't let you risk your life on a slim chance like this. He might have left guards there.'

Taylor checked his guns, then gave Morgan an even wider grin. 'I ain't doing this on my lonesome, Uncle. You're coming with me. If you can shoot as well as you can talk, I reckon we got a fighting chance of survival.'

Morgan's jaw dropped. 'Oh dear Lord! You want both of us to get killed! I should have known that by the way you handled that herd of Cheyenne braves.'

Taylor unlocked the door. 'C'mon! You're too tough for any of those critters to kill.'

Both men slid out on to the boardwalk. Morgan locked the door behind them and they started towards the large house, which did appear to be deserted.

Yet with every step they both silently acknowledged that appearances could be and often were deceptive. Morgan checked his own weapon and wondered whether his two years of living in this border town might just be coming to an end.

Taylor paused as they reached the Cartwheel. He looked over the swing doors at the interior of the saloon and the handful of souls who still remained within its four walls. Two bar girls who had seen better days more than a decade earlier still tried to ply their trade as the remaining men drank what was left of their money away. An acrid odour filled Taylor's nostrils. It was the unpleasant aroma of stale liquor and drying blood.

'You know any of them in there, Pop?' Taylor

asked quietly. 'Any of them belong to Carter?'

Morgan moved closer to the wood and peered over the top of the swing doors. His eyes darted around the saloon.

'None of them belongs to Carter, Ethan.'

'Good!' Taylor nodded, pushed the doors apart and led the way into the large room. The sawdust beneath their boots was stale and stank. Taylor noticed a large portion of the sawdust which was stained with what appeared to be gore. 'See that, Pop?'

'I see it,' Morgan confirmed. 'Looks like somebody had an argument with a six-shooter and lost.'

Both men headed slowly towards the bartender who leaned on the bar counter as he fought off the desire to sleep which dogged him. The sound of erratic snoring greeted the two new customers.

Morgan looked at his partner. He was unsure as to why they had entered the saloon when they were originally headed for Carter's house.

'What's going on, pally?'

'Information, Pop,' Taylor winked. 'We need information.'

Only the eyes of the two bar girls took any notice. They saw fresh pickings and began to circle the two men like vultures waiting for the right time to strike.

'You want a good time, stranger?' a female with red hair asked Taylor. Her fingers started to investigate his lean, muscular torso. 'My name's Katie!'

'I'm called Francie. I'll give you a better deal than she can,' the bar girl with dark hair interrupted. 'I'll give you the best time you ever had!'

Taylor and Morgan continued towards the bar.

As they reached the long wooden counter the girls went to either side of them. Their hands began to search the men for any signs of interest. Both men tried to ignore the small fingers as they rubbed and squeezed what they found two inches below their belt buckles.

'Hey!' Morgan shouted at the bartender. There was a hint of excitement in his voice. 'Wake up, barkeep!'

The bartender pushed himself upright and stared through blurred eyes at the two new customers. He gave a sigh and walked to them.

'What'll it be?

'Two whiskeys,' Taylor answered quickly.

'What about us?' Katie asked, continuing to massage Taylor's pants. 'We got a thirst bigger than yours.'

Taylor smiled at her. 'I really ain't got time for any pleasure, little lady.'

'I want a drink!' she shouted up at his right ear.

'And me!' Francie joined in in equal volume.

Taylor pulled a few coins from his shirt pocket and placed them on the bar counter as the bartender placed two glasses of whiskey before

Morgan and himself.

'And a bottle with a cork,' he added.

Morgan leaned against his parner. 'I thought we were going to do something else, Ethan!'

'Trust me, Pop!' Taylor swallowed his whiskey, picked up two more glasses and plucked the bottle off the wet counter. He looked around and saw the darkest corner of the saloon. 'Let's take the gals over there and give them a few drinks, Uncle.'

'What?' Morgan rolled his eyes. He trailed Taylor who seemed far more capable of walking with a hand over his manhood than he was. 'I sure wish I knew what you were doing, nephew of mine.'

Taylor sat down and offered a chair to one of the bar girls. Katie dropped on his lap and giggled.

'Your mouth is saying no but I feel something saying yes!' Katie said into his ear.

Taylor pulled the cork with his teeth, spat it at the floor, then filled all their glasses. He was getting hot and had to try and remain focused on what he and Morgan were going to attempt. It was not easy.

Morgan reached a chair and somehow managed to sit down. The female who had already succeeded in awakening something he had long thought dead jumped on his knee and started to wiggle.

'Hey!' Francie proclaimed. 'You ain't as old as

them white whiskers would make folks think! Is that what I reckon it is, old-timer?'

Morgan cleared his throat. 'That's my pipe, young lady!'

Francie raised her plucked eyebrows and then reached into the breast pocket of Morgan's coat. She pulled out the pipe and waved it around.

'Then what's this?'

'Ethan?' Morgan gulped.

Taylor raised a hand and silenced his nervous companion. He tried to look at the female who was attempting to eat his neck and face.

'Where's all Carter's men?'

Katie pulled her lips from his face. 'One of them is dead out back. Brad Green blew him away.'

'Dead?' Taylor glanced at Morgan.

'Yep. Jack Wright was Carter's top gun.' Francie joined in the story. 'He picked on a few of the others and Brad just gunned him down. It was so funny.'

Taylor and Morgan glanced at one another. They were stunned that the well-paid gunfighters were already turning upon one another.

'We heard a shot coming from Carter's house after the rest of his boys went there.' The female on Morgan's lap laughed as she continued to wriggle. 'I think Carter shot Brad.'

'That'll teach him!' Taylor grinned.

'He won't do that again,' Morgan sighed.

'Damn right!' Katie moved her bottom slightly and reached down between Taylor's legs. He tried to stand but she was far better at this sort of thing than he would ever be. He gave a cough, then reached for the whiskey bottle again and took a swig.

'Five bucks,' Francie whispered into Morgan's ear.

'Did you happen to see who it was that rode out of town a few minutes ago, Katie?' Taylor asked.

'Carter,' Katie replied.

'And his boys,' Francie chipped in.

Taylor swallowed hard. 'All of them?'

'As good as.' Katie had started to undo the buttons which held his pants together.

Using every ounce of his strength, Taylor stood with the female in his arms. He turned and placed her on the table. He then lifted Francie off Morgan's lap and placed her next to the red-haired girl.

'What's going on?' a surprised Katie enquired.

Taylor touched her face. 'Sorry. Pop and me have business to sort out.'

'We got business to finish upstairs, big guy!' Francie said loudly. She picked up the bottle and started to consume its contents.

'I'm sorry,' Taylor shrugged.

'You taste pretty good,' Katie smiled coyly. 'Come back when you've the time.'

'I might just do that!' Taylor handed the girls two five-dollar bills, hauled the older man off the chair and started to drag him out of the Cartwheel. Morgan staggered as he fumbled with his pants.

'Not so fast, pally,' Morgan complained.

'What?'

'I can hardly walk here, pally! Slow up!'

Taylor continued to lead the older man along the street towards the mansion on the edge of San Remas. Neither of them knew for sure whether it was deserted. They would find out soon enough.

# TWELVE

Their experience had begun to show. They moved like phantoms down the long street using every scrap of shadow and avoiding each of the street lanterns which might reveal their whereabouts to the eyes of those who they knew would betray them. The two ex-military men had done this before and knew that it was not a game they could afford to lose. Failure meant death and that was a forfeit they did not wish to pay.

The people who were still on the streets of San Remas did not seem to notice either Taylor or Morgan as the pair moved unseen towards their goal.

The saloons and brothels seemed to be doing their usual trade and men moved aimlessly between the centres of both kinds of escapism.

Scott Taylor was first to reach the well-constructed wall of the courtyard which surrounded the even better-built house itself. He rested his sweat-soaked shirt back against the cool adobe wall and watched as Morgan slid from the shadows and joined him.

The older man was panting slightly. It was his only concession to age. He rested a hand upon one of Taylor's broad shoulders until he managed to get his second wind.

Torch- and lantern-light cascaded from the open gates in the wall around the corner from where they rested. It was a warning that they were now within mere yards of possible death. They had to remain alert and, like mountain cats, ready to react with the blink of an eye.

Both men listened and tried to hear whether there were still guards present within the grounds of Carter's luxurious home.

'You hear anybody, Pop?' Taylor whispered.

Morgan shook his head in silent reply.

'If we come up against trouble we have to shoot our way out of it.' Taylor drew one of his Colts, cocked its hammer and held it at hip level. He began to walk.

Morgan followed.

The sand muffled their footsteps from anyone who might be still within the confines of the high wall. The two men moved in the darkness like human shadows. If any eyes tried to see them they would be unlucky.

Taylor was first to turn into the courtyard. He threw himself into the cover of tall bushes. Morgan defied his own age and did almost exactly the same.

They paused for a few seemingly endless moments until their eyes adjusted to the flickering torchlight. Taylor tapped his friend's arm and began to lead the way through the foliage towards the house itself.

When they spied the rear door swaying in the slight desert breeze, they ran to it. Both men went straight into the house and stopped against its tiled walls. Taylor pointed the barrel of his gun at the floor. It was made of highly polished tiles. Morgan knew what his partner meant. Tiles like these tended to magnify the sound of anything which passed across them.

They thought for a few moments as their eyes surveyed the interior of the large house.

There were rooms behind them which appeared to lead nowhere. Their doors were dowdy by comparison to those which adorned the rest of the mansion.

Morgan leaned into his comrade. 'Servants' quarters?'

Taylor thought about the suggestion. It made sense. Then another thought raced into his mind. Carter and his henchmen might have ridden out for the fortress, but servants would more than likely still be inside the big building.

What if they were loyal to Carter?

What if they were armed and willing to die to protect their employer's property?

'C'mon,' Taylor said.

The pair walked as quietly as they could along the tiled floor away from the servants' quarters. The main living-room seemed almost bare. Few objects, apart from chairs and a table, stood in the vast area.

'There!' Morgan pointed to his left. Taylor turned and looked at where his friend's finger was aimed.

Both had seen many staircases in their time. Neither man had ever seen one like the one they were looking at now.

It was wide. It curved to the right. It had marble adornments to both sides and the most expensive-looking carpet stretching from its base right up to the upper floor. This was where Carter must have spent a lot of his ill-gotten gains, both men thought at exactly the same moment.

'That's a mighty fine set of steps there, pally,' Morgan said.

'Waste of money!' Taylor commented.

Morgan led the way up the stairs. His companion trailed him by a few steps. Both held their guns at their hips, ready to use them at any moment.

The upper floor was even more impressive than the lower. Again it was clear that Cody Carter liked to spend money. Whether it belonged to him or not, he obviously liked spending it.

Taylor went straight for a large desk near the far wall as Morgan just drifted around the room in search of a safe. The younger man holstered his gun, knelt and started to pull the drawers open one by one. Each was filled with papers which seemed to be nothing more than miscellaneous bills and receipts. Whether they were genuine or not mattered little to Taylor. He knew they had nothing to do with why he and his partner were here.

Unlike the others, the top left drawer was locked.

Taylor struck a match and studied the well-made brass lock, then blew the flame out. He stood and ran his hands across the desk until they came across a long stiletto. It was clear that it was not a weapon but a letter-opener. He tested the blade's strength, then pushed it at the top of the drawer. Taylor carefully levered it until the lock gave and he was able to slide the drawer towards him. Taylor had been right when he guessed that there was only one reason for this particular drawer to have been secured.

There were only a dozen or so letters. He lifted them all out of the pine rectangle, walked to the large window and used the balcony lantern to read them. His eyebrows rose.

'This is it, Pop!' Taylor said.

The older man raced across the room. He took the letters that Taylor handed him. One after another the same name occurred. A name that they both knew only too well.

'General Theo Jackson!' Morgan said in utter shock.

'So he's the traitor who's been selling us all down the river!' Taylor almost growled as he felt his fury rising.

'Look at this, pally!' Morgan raised one of the items of correspondence and held it beneath Taylor's nose. 'This gives the details of how much money Carter has been paying the bastard!'

'Now we have our rope.' Taylor carefully folded the letters and slid them inside his shirt. 'Now we can hang Cody Carter!'

'And Jackson!' Morgan added.

The two men turned and were about to leave the room when they saw a light from below cast up the high staircase wall. Someone had lit either a lantern or candles downstairs. The eerie silhouette of a man with a scatter-gun moved up the wall as the figure ascended.

Morgan looked at Taylor. 'Who the hell is that?'

'Whoever it is the varmint's loaded for bear!' Taylor whispered back.

Morgan went to hide behind the desk when he felt the firm grip of Taylor's left hand on his collar. He was dragged out on to the balcony.

Taylor drew one of his guns and cocked its hammer. 'See if there's a way down from here that means we don't have to jump!'

'Jump?' Morgan repeated the word before gulping. 'I ain't been able to jump since before you were born.'

'Look!' Taylor snapped, 'if there ain't a way I'll have to kill this joker.'

Morgan ran along the balcony which stretched the entire length of the building's façade. For all his desperation he could not find a way down from the balcony which did not require dropping the twenty feet to the sandy yard. He shook his head frantically and looked back at his partner.

'We gotta go back through the room, pally.'

Taylor gritted his teeth. 'Damn it all!'

The man with the scatter-gun was about forty with a long thin moustache hanging limply from under his nose. His eyes flashed around the room as his shaking hands gripped the huge gun. He was no guard, just a servant from across the border. A man who was misguided in his loyalty to the person who paid his wages.

'Is anyone there?' The timid Mexican managed to call out when he had reached the room. He

107

prayed that no one would reply. 'Hello?'

Taylor looked around the edge of the long velvet drape at the man who was venturing deeper into the huge room. Taylor was not afraid of the man himself but knew only too well how perilous scatter-guns could be when loaded with the right kind of buckshot.

'Go back!' Taylor shouted from his relatively safe position. He did not want to kill someone he believed to be nothing more than a terrified servant, but he knew that sometimes frightened men were more dangerous than brave ones. 'Drop that gun!'

The man stopped walking, raised the scatter-gun and without hesitation fired both barrels in the direction of the voice. The sound was deafening. The massive drape crashed down in front of Taylor.

Debris showered over him as he crouched.

'Get going!' Taylor warned again.

But the Mexican had already reloaded the scatter-gun and had raised it. Both men squinted as the night air moved the dust between them like shadowy ghosts.

Taylor bit his lip. He knew that there was only one way out of this place for Morgan. They had to return the way they had come. Unlike himself the older man could not leap from the balcony without sustaining injury.

The Mexican was now closer. He had found courage in the fearful shots he had just unleashed. He raised the double-barrelled weapon and aimed at Taylor.

There was no alternative for Taylor. He fanned the hammer of his Colt and let a single shot loose from the .45's barrel.

His bullet caught the man high in the shoulder, sending him cartwheeling on the marble-tiled floor. He slid across its polished surface into a wall. With the impact of colliding with the wall his index finger jerked both of the big gun's triggers into action.

Again the scatter-gun spewed out its buckshot. A plume of white lightning lit up the room for the briefest of moments.

This time it was the ceiling above them all which took the full impact of the gun's force.

Plaster showered down in massive chunks. The choking dust clouded the vision of the injured man who lay clutching his shoulder on the floor. He did not see the two men who ran towards him.

As both men reached their fallen victim Morgan grabbed the barrel of the scatter-gun from his grip and tossed it across the room.

'Do not kill me, *señor*!' the man begged. 'I am nothing!'

Taylor and Morgan did not say a word. They

continued running until they had reached the courtyard and beyond.

They had bigger prey on their minds.

# THIRTEEN

The morning sun had risen two hours earlier. Its heat grew with every mile the horsemen covered on their dogged journey to the fortress. Cody Carter led the riders down across the sandy dunes until they reached the flat land which led to the fortress. Smoke still rose into the blue cloudless sky. Its black plumes seemed almost to equal the blackness of the hearts of the approaching gunfighters. But there was something else in the sky besides the smoke.

Each of the men in Carter's band of killers suddenly saw the circling vultures and knew what lay ahead. Death had drawn the massive birds to feast upon the flesh of the fallen.

The fourteen horsemen had ridden all night to reach this remote place and discover the truth for themselves, but they had not thought what failure meant out here in the ocean of sand.

Carter pushed his hat back on his head and stared up at the birds floating on the warm thermals. Then he saw those who had already landed. They were ripping bodies apart with their massive curved beaks as their talons kept the corpses anchored.

'Oh my God!' Carter muttered.

'Pop Parker was right,' Kid Dynamite said.

'Yeah,' Carter sighed heavily.

The gunfighters trailed their boss down towards the wooden walls. Their lathered-up mounts could smell the water within the boundaries of Fort Briggs and started to increase pace. Carter was first to reach the wrecked gates. He hauled rein and stopped his mount.

The vultures barely noticed the horsemen until Carter drew his gun and started to shoot them. He had killed three of their number before the rest rose up into the air and flew to join the others circling the dead Indians.

The riders could barely look at what was left of the bodies as they rode into the parade ground behind their leader. The corpses had been torn apart by the hungry vultures. One remaining corpse still retained a reconizably human shape.

Carter inhaled. His guts had turned even before he dismounted and allowed his horse to drink from one of the troughs near the fort's well. He stared across the sand at the body and then snapped his fingers at his men.

'Fill them canteens!' Carter ordered. 'Then grain the horses. We need these nags to get us back to town!'

One by one they stepped down from their horses. But it was Kid Dynamite who kept close to Carter as his fellow gunfighters filled their canteens from the well and allowed their thirsty mounts to drink. He could see the confused expression carved into Carter's features as he looked at severed limbs scattered all around the sand.

'Is that meant to be Taylor, boss?' the Kid asked.

Carter said nothing.

He started to walk towards the torso and head. It was the largest part of the body still intact. When he had reached it he leaned over. Even now the stench of death was strong and as the sun grew hotter, its acrid aroma increased. Carter turned and covered his face with his hands.

'This could be anybody,' Carter said. 'The Cheyenne made a good job of burning the dumb critter.'

'What's that poking out of his pocket?' The Kid walked to the body and knelt. He pushed a gloved hand into the pants pocket and pulled out the scrap of paper Morgan had planted there. He shook it until the paper unfolded and then gave it to Carter.

'This is Taylor's orders!' Carter said after reading it. 'The ones that he was given at the Adobe Wells railhead!'

'Then I guess that it must be Taylor.' Kid Dynamite rubbed his gloves on his shirt in a vain bid to rid them of the smell of decay. 'Besides, the critter I tried to bushwhack was dressed in the same clothes! I recall seeing them through the buffalo gun's sights.'

'You sure of that?'

The Kid nodded. 'Damn sure!'

'Excellent!' Carter smiled, turned and started towards the rest of his men and horses. There was a spring in his step which belied the fact that, a large man, he had ridden all night. 'Fill them canteens, feed the horses and then we'll head back to town.'

'I'm hungry, boss,' Hume said. 'How come the horses get to eat and we don't?'

'Then eat some jerky,' Carter yelled. 'Just quit whining!'

Pete Smith was standing away from the rest of the men. He was looking almost directly into the sun.

'You'll go blind looking at the sun like that, Pete,' Carter said as he pulled his canteens from his saddle horn and gave them to one of the other men. 'C'mon! I for one don't want to be here a minute longer than called for.'

Smith turned.

'I ain't looking at the sun, Mr Carter.'

Carter paused. 'Then what are you looking at?'

Smith raised a hand and pointed. 'Him!'

Cody Carter screwed up his eyes and tried to see what Smith was pointing at. The bright sun made it impossible.

'You looking at the buzzards?'

'He's got feathers OK,' Smith shrugged. 'But he sure ain't a buzzard, Mr Carter.'

'What are you talking about?' Carter strode across the sand and stood next to Smith. He shielded his eyes with his hands and then saw what had caught Smith's attention. He reached into his coat pocket and pulled out a small pair of binoculars. Carter looked through them and tuned the focus until he could see the paint upon the face of the man beneath the war bonnet on the high ridge.

'What is it, boss?' the Kid called out.

Carter lowered his hands, returned the binoculars to his pocket and scratched his jaw. He pulled a cigar from his silk vest pocket, bit off its tip and pushed it into the corner of his mouth. He continued to look up at the ridge which was directly across from the destroyed gates. He struck a match with his thumbnail and then sucked in its flame. Smoke drifted from his lips as the large man watched the curious Kid approaching.

'What's wrong, boss?' the Kid asked. 'What you seen out there?'

'Red Eagle!' Carter answered through a cloud of cigar smoke.

'How come you don't look happy?' Kid Dynamite could not understand the concern he saw in his boss. 'He's on our side. Right?'

Carter pulled the cigar from his mouth. 'I ain't so sure any more, Kid. I just got me a bad feeling. He's still painted for war.'

'But he's on his lonesome.'

'I doubt it, Kid.'

The Kid looked at his boss. 'But you give him a whole lotta whiskey and the best carbines money can buy.'

A cold shiver traced Carter's spine. 'That's what I'm worried about. Let's get out of here as fast as we can, Kid. I got me an inkling that Red Eagle ain't our pal no more.'

'Why not?'

Carter turned on his heels and dragged Smith and the Kid with him back to the horses and the rest of the men. He raised his arms and started to shout at the top of his voice.

'Forget feeding the horses, boys! We're getting back on the trail right now!'

The men secured their canteens to the saddle horns and mounted in quick succession. Carter turned the head of his mount around and checked his own rifle.

'Make sure your damn rifles are ready for action!' Carter commanded. 'We might have to use them if I'm right.'

Kid Dynamite drew his horse next to his boss and held two primed dynamite sticks in his left hand. He was grinning broadly as he leaned across to Carter. 'You gotta cigar I can borrow?'

Carter pulled his cigar from his mouth. 'Will this do, Kid?'

The Kid nodded.

'Yep! That'll do just fine!'

# FOURTEEN

Like men with the Devil on their backs, the fourteen riders moved out from the relative safety of the fortress and started to retrace their tracks. Carter knew that something was wrong but could not quite get to grips with exactly what that was. In all his encounters with the Cheyenne he had been in control. He had managed to stir their hatred for all whites except himself and his men by bribing them with more than enough hard liquor and the very best Winchesters he could get his hands on.

Chief Red Eagle had been easily manipulated and during the previous year had attacked and killed more than a hundred innocent settlers, leaving their land for Carter to buy for a few cents in the dollar.

Carter rode with Kid Dynamite at his side along the sandy trail towards the deep dry creek that led along Blood River to the distant San Remas. The

118

riders had not felt any worries when they had been heading to the fort but now the high ridges to either side of their horses gave them cause for concern.

The creek was more than two miles in length. Sagebrush grew in the shadows where the vicious sun never managed to reach. The riders started to draw closer to one another as though there was safety in numbers.

Back at the fort, before they set out for town, Carter had noted that Red Eagle had vanished from the top of the ridge. Now his mind kept asking the same haunting question.

Why had the chief not ridden down to talk with him?

It was the first time that had ever happened. Another question troubled him.

Had he turned the once peaceful Indian and what remained of his warriors into ruthless killers whom he could no longer control?

The second thought frightened him more than the first. Carter knew that he had created a monster for his own gain but now he feared that the Indian was a monster who would turn upon his master. Lines of sweat started to run from his hatband down his face until his shirt collar was soaked. Carter knew that it was not the baking sun, which was now nearly directly overhead, that was causing him to melt. It was fear of the unknown.

Carter kept looking to both sides of the ridges which flanked them. Every sinew in his body told him that he and his men were in trouble.

'Keep up!' Carter shouted over his shoulder at his men.

The Kid still held the two sticks of explosives firmly. He had trimmed their fuses down to a mere two inches in length. For most men it would have been suicidal to work with such short fuses but the Kid was an expert. He knew that once he touched the fuses with the smouldering cigar between his teeth he had only ten seconds before they exploded.

For Kid Dynamite that was an eternity.

Scott Taylor moved through the hardware store silently as Morgan served his customers. It was nearly eleven and they had been working solidly for three hours. He had lost count of how many times his colleague had introduced him as his nephew. Eventually the last of them left the store.

Taylor dropped the two boxes he had carried in from the storeroom and went to the side of the older man.

'This is driving me loco!'

Morgan raised a white eyebrow. 'I know, but we have to keep up the masquerade for a little while longer. These townsfolk think we are what we claim to be and in a way that's exactly what we are until we have a chance to get our hands on Carter.'

'We have the legal authority to take Carter dead or alive but doing it without getting ourselves killed in the process is another thing.' Taylor shook his head. 'And what if that Mexican servant gives Carter a description of us? There can't be many folks like us around.'

Morgan nodded.

'They won't get back to town for hours.'

'I still think that we'd be better served heading out after them and trying to get the better of them out in the desert,' Taylor said. 'I hate this waiting around.'

'We talked this over last night,' Morgan argued. 'We don't want to increase the odds against us.'

'What you mean?'

'We don't want to have the desert against us as well, do we, pally?' Morgan was smiling again.

Taylor shook his head.

'I'll go alone.'

'But there are over a dozen of them, pally.'

'I'm going to the livery and saddling that mule you call a horse, partner,' Taylor said firmly. 'I'd rather fight it out in the desert than here in San Remas. We ain't sure how many of these folks voted for him and don't know that he's a ruthless crook. Nope. It'll be better to take him out there.'

Morgan said nothing. He removed his white

apron and placed it on top of a stack of horse blankets before moving to the doors. He closed and bolted them and then pulled down the blinds.

'You coming with me?' Taylor asked.

'Somebody has to make sure you don't get yourself killed.'

The high ridges seemed to be getting closer to the horsemen as they continued on beneath the noon sun. Each of the riders kept his eyes on the red sandy rises as if waiting for the Grim Reaper to make an appearance at any moment. Their trepidation was not too unwarranted. Cody Carter led his small troop along the floor of the dry creek towards the river, which they could now see.

'Another mile or and we can water the nags, boss,' Hume called out.

'Yep,' Carter reluctantly agreed.

'You OK now, Mr Carter?' Pete Smith enquired as he rode alongside the Kid and his grim-faced employer. 'You sure bin on edge for the longest while.'

Suddenly it was as if each of them had the same premonition at the very same moment. They did not hear anything but they knew the hairs on the napes of their necks did not stand on end for nothing.

As though drawn by some unknown force, Carter tilted his head slightly and looked up at the ridge to his left. He gasped. At least thirty mounted Cheyenne had silently appeared on the top of the ridge as if from nowhere. Each carried a Winchester and was painted for battle. He turned to tell the Kid when another line of warriors rode their ponies up on to the very crown of the opposite ridge.

'Kid!' Carter gasped fearfully.

Kid Dynamite sucked on his cigar until its tip glowed like a firefly.

'I seen 'em, boss.'

'Boss!' One of the riders behind them called out. 'What's happening?'

'Keep riding!' Carter ordered them all loudly.

'It's OK! That's Red Eagle, boss,' Hume informed his paymaster.

Carter attempted to clear his throat. It was a pointless exercise. It felt as though he had swallowed a cactus. He went to spit but that too failed. Fear was like a hangman's noose, it hurt real bad.

'Easy, boss,' the Kid told the older man. 'They ain't done nothing yet.'

'Give them time.' Once more Carter turned his head and stared at the pony riders above them to the left and then to the right. His heart began to pound like a war drum inside his sweat-sodden shirt. They all had the Winchesters he had given them resting on their naked thighs as they kept pace with the gunfighters.

123

'They look kinda mean,' a confused Smith surmised.

'What's the matter with Red Eagle?' Carter begged the Kid for answers he himself could not find. 'What's that savage bastard think he's doing?'

The Kid looked ahead and then back at Carter. 'We're closing in on the river fast. If they're gonna do something it'll be anytime now.'

The words were like a tombstone around Carter's neck. He turned on his saddle and shouted at his men. 'Speed up! Let's see what they're gonna do!'

With almost military precision the gunfighters spurred and doubled their pace. They drew closer together and allowed the Kid to see a place where he could throw one of his deadly sticks of dynamite. After igniting the fuse the young rider tossed the stick as high as he could.

It exploded just below the top of the ridge. Sand flew in all directions but the pony riders continued their high pursuit.

Carter's men increased their pace. Their mounts ate up the sand beneath their hoofs. The Cheyenne's unshod mounts matched them stride for stride.

'What we gonna do?' Hume cried out.

'Keep riding!' Carter replied as he whipped the shoulders of his horse with the lengths of his reins. 'Once we hit the river all we have to do is cross it.

There's plenty of cover over there.'

Carter was correct. An array of tree trunks and boulders had been washed up on the opposite side of Blood River over countless decades. All they had to do was cross the stretch of water to reach it.

They heard Red Eagle call out to his braves as they thundered along the crests of the ridges above the galloping gunmen.

Suddenly, like soldier ants, the warriors swarmed down from their high vantage points towards Carter and his men. The war cries needed no explanation to any of those who now used their spurs savagely as they attempted to put distance between themselves and the Indians.

The majority of the warriors intercepted the trailing riders.

Agonized cries rang out along the dry river-bed from the tail of the group. They were enveloped by the dust of the Cheyenne.

The creek-bed echoed with the sound of rifle fire as the braves' Winchesters blasted. The gunfighters who survived the onslaught of bullets fell as flashing knives and stabbing lances lashed out with equal barbarity. Blood now flowed unchecked from the dead and dying gunmen.

Now only seven of the gunfighters remained. They forged on to the river which, like a night-marish dream, seemed never to get any closer.

Red Eagle had acted as Carter's puppet for too

long but it had taken the death of his only son back at the fortress the previous day to sober him up and make him see who his true enemy really was.

They say that revenge has a bitter taste. But it was one which Red Eagle was willing to savour.

The Cheyenne chief screamed his venomous fury at the top of his lungs and led his regrouped warriors after the fleeing riders. He had yet to unleash the bullets from the gleaming rifle he held aloft as he chased his prey.

These he intended to save for the man he blamed for his brutal loss.

They drove through a cloud of swirling dust. Carter was first to reach the banks of the river. He did not pause for even a second. His spurs and reins forced the animal beneath him to ride straight into the dark-red water. Within the length of the horse's long stride he found the water up to his knees. Now his horse was swimming and all he could do was hang on.

The current was strong but his mount was stronger.

With wide, desperate eyes he looked back as his other hired guns followed him into the river. Only Kid Dynamite held back for a few endless seconds.

Just before his own mount had reached the water's edge the Kid lifted one of the deadly explosive sticks to his mouth and to the tip of the cigar gripped firmly between his teeth. The glowing end touched the fuse and it started to hiss like a crazed sidewinder.

With every ounce of his youthful power he tossed the stick at the approaching warriors, spun his horse around and then drove on into the fast-flowing waves.

No sooner had his mount entered the blood-red water than the dynamite stick exploded behind him.

The blast went high and wide. Debris showered over the water like fiery rain. As the Kid hung on to the saddle horn of his swimming horse he glanced over his shoulder and saw the mayhem behind him.

At least a dozen of the Cheyenne had been either killed or maimed. They had been torn to bits by the blinding eruption but the rest kept coming.

Red Eagle still had the scent of his prey in his flared nostrils. Only Carter's death would quench his thirst for retribution.

# FIFTEEN

Fountains of white spray more than ten feet high flew into the midday air as the seven horsemen ploughed across the wide river. Winchester bullets chased and found them. Only the churned-up water gave them any protection from their pursuers' lethal rifles. George Hume had barely reached the centre of the river when he buckled as the hot lead ripped through him from a half-dozen Cheyenne rifles.

Blood exploded from the multitude of wounds. The gunfighter twisted on his saddle and then fell into the fast-swirling current. Before Kid Dynamite reached him Hume had vanished into the water and was washed away. The Kid dragged his reins to his chest and dug his spurs into the horse's flesh. The animal leapt into the deepest part of the river with its master hanging half-submerged at its side. Bullets whizzed all around the young rider like

128

buzzsaws, but the Kid kept low.

Two of Carter's other men also were riddled with bullets as their mounts bobbed up in the waves created by the great numbers of fleeing animals. Dexter and Franks were names that would be forgotten sooner than most. They floated away like rag dolls in the red waters of the aptly named Blood River.

Kid Dynamite jabbed a spur into his horse as the bodies passed within inches of him. With water hitting him full in the face he tried to see the Cheyenne but failed. He saw their bullets though, as they tore into his saddle narrowly missing his right hand on the saddle horn. His horse gave a pitiful noise and began to slow. Then he saw the blood surrounding him as the wounded horse continued to swim.

About twenty yards ahead Carter managed to spur his mount for the last few yards before its hoofs found the embankment. With rifle shots echoing all around he felt his animal buckle and fall. He hit the ground and rolled away from the shaking creature. Carter was exhausted but still capable of hauling his own rifle from its saddle scabbard and dragging himself to the cover of a large sun-bleached tree trunk.

Carter crawled behind it as more and more bullets ripped away at it. He lay staring over the brittle bark of the tree at what remained of his once powerful force. A force that was now reduced to a mere three men.

Beyond them, the Cheyenne kept on firing the brand-new weaponry with which he had supplied them. His mind tried to reason with what was happening but it could not. He had no knowledge of why Red Eagle had turned on him and that ignorance tortured his addled mind.

Bedraggled men and horses reached the river-bank. Smith and Holden dropped to the ground and led their mounts away as Kid Dynamite eventually rode up on to the wet sand atop his own injured horse.

Carter watched as the youngster pulled his heroic buffalo gun from beneath the saddle and then grabbed his saddlebags. A mere beat of his heart saw the horse fall. The Kid ran and leapt down beside his boss.

'You OK, boss?' the Kid asked as he opened his bags and pulled out a box of large bullets for the single-shot weapon and a handful of dynamite sticks. He spread them out beside him. 'Boss?'

Cody Carter just stared in disbelief into nowhere. He did not answer the question because he had not heard it. All he could hear was the war chants of the Cheyenne and the venom of their Winchesters.

His mind had broken. Now all he seemed capable of was to fumble for his gun in its hidden

130

holster beneath his left armpit.

'Boss?' The Kid looked hard at the face beside him. It was not the face he had once feared. Now it was a pathetic mockery of a once strong man's countenance.

'Taylor!' Carter muttered. 'He's dead. Taylor's dead so everything will be fine.'

'I know Taylor's dead, boss.' The Kid was stunned by the confused figure beside him. 'We all know that.'

Carter smiled and went to rise. 'Let's go!'

Kid Dynamite grabbed Carter's shoulders and pushed him back down on to the sand. Carter went to rise again. This time the Kid was forced to clench his fist and land it upon Carter's chin as hard as he could.

Carter's eyes rolled. He slumped over.

Smith crawled to the side of the Kid. 'You hit him! You hit the boss, Kid!'

'I had to! He's gone loco!'

Suddenly bullets came at them from every rifle still in the hands of the Cheyenne. The Kid looked up and saw that half of the warriors were riding through the rough water towards them. He grabbed his buffalo gun and handed sticks of explosives to his frightened comrade.

'What the hell you giving these to me for?' Smith gulped.

The Kid cocked the giant rifle in his hands and

held it to his shoulder. He closed one eye and focused through its sights.

'You throw them one at a time and I'll shoot the damn things!'

Smith nodded. 'OK, Kid. If'n ya say so.'

'Now!' the Kid snapped. He stared down the long barrel. 'Throw the damn thing!'

Pete Smith hurled the stick at the river and the approaching braves. As it almost reached the centre of the river water, the Kid squeezed the trigger of his trusty rifle. The bullet burst from the buffalo gun with deafening fury. It hit the explosive stick a split second later.

The explosion sent braves and water erupting into the noon air. A whirlwind of smoke rotated like a small tornado as body parts of men and horses scattered on the embankment.

Billy Holden crawled beside the last of his comrades and looked hard at them. He held his guns in his hands and started to fire over the top of the tree trunk.

Smith picked up another dynamite stick. 'Again?'

'Again!' Kid Dynamite nodded.

Smith leaned back and hurled it as far as he could. Again it almost reached the middle of the raging river.

The Kid's unerring marksmanship found its target once more.

132

The explosion was bigger than the previous one.

Holden leaned back and looked across at the Kid. 'They're still coming, Kid.'

'I know they are.'

# SIXTEEN

This was where the prairie gave way to the desert. A few yards from the foot of the high mesas the sagebrush dwindled to nothing more than sand beneath the blazing sun. But it was not the satanic scenery that caused the two horsemen to rein in. It was the noise which rippled through the dry air and greeted them.

Even from more than ten miles away from the bloodshed, the hideous sound of the ferocious battle rang out and reached the ears of the two riders.

Scott Taylor and Josh Morgan rode up between the crest of two mountain peaks and drew rein. Red dust drifted from the hoofs of their tired horses. They steadied the skittish animals and then studied the land far below them. Taylor pointed at the river which cut through the hard rock on its way to the desert and beyond.

Morgan moved his horse closer to his partner's. 'There, pally! See them?'

Taylor had seen the unmistakable evidence of the still raging battle long before Morgan had. He looked at the older man and bit his lip.

'What are Indians fighting Carter and his gang for? I thought they were bosom buddies.'

Morgan sighed. 'That don't look like buddies having a little disagreement to me. That's serious, pally. Real serious.'

'You still want to carry on?' Taylor asked. He quenched his thirst with a mouthful of warm water from his canteen. 'I figure there ain't gonna be a lot left of any of them when the gunsmoke lifts.'

'We have a job to finish,' Morgan said. 'We have to head on down there and arrest whoever is left of Carter and his cronies.'

Taylor was surprised by Morgan's conviction. 'By the time we get there I reckon there won't be anyone on Carter's side left alive.'

'We still have to try,' Morgan said. 'Our job is to arrest Carter and as many of his cronies as we can. Or just pick up their stinking carcasses and take them to the nearest law.'

Taylor shook his head slightly. 'It'll take more than an hour to reach there, Morgan.'

Morgan looked straight down at where the river was closest to their high vantage point. A wry knowing smile crossed his face as he turned back to face his companion.

'Maybe not.'

Taylor raised an eyebrow. He knew that Morgan was a cunning man who had only lived so long because he was smarter than most.

'What do you mean by that, old man?'

'You'll see.' Morgan gathered his reins and tapped his spurs to urge his mount on its downward journey towards the river. The horse carefully descended the sandy slope as its master leaned back against the saddle cantle.

'What does that mean?' Taylor pulled his reins to his side and guided his mount after Morgan's. There was no reply, only the curled finger which encouraged the younger man to follow.

A cloud of scarlet dust drifted out across the desert as the pair of secret service men made their way down towards the river and the heat, which only the Devil could have truly tolerated.

Taylor knew that Morgan had an idea. That was enough.

As the fight raged on, Cody Carter blinked and then opened his eyes to consciousness. The ruthless man tried to speak, but his loose teeth and sore jaw stopped him. He raised his hands and cupped his face. Then he felt a hand on his shoulder and looked through his fingers at the concerned features of the Kid.

136

'You OK now, Mr Carter?'

'Did you hit me, Kid?' Carter growled as best he could.

'I had to punch you, boss,' Kid Dynamite replied. 'You were acting kinda crazy. You tried to stand up even though them Indians had our range. I just had to stop you getting yourself killed.'

'I don't remember anything,' Carter admitted. 'What's happening now?'

'We've bin holding them off for nearly an hour,' the Kid said. 'But I'm running out of dynamite.'

Smith and Holden crawled to their paymaster. 'The Kid has killed half of them but they still keep attacking,' Holden said.

'Red Eagle just won't quit, boss,' Smith added. 'We ain't got a lot of bullets left.'

Carter ignored his pain and ran his fingers through his thinning hair as he straightened up. The rifle shots were still raining in on their hiding-place. He screwed up his eyes and spat blood at the sand, then glanced tentatively over the scarred tree trunk.

'We have to get out of here, boys,' he said firmly. 'And the sooner the better.'

'That ain't so easy,' Smith said quickly.

Carter grabbed Smith's bandanna and dragged the gunfighter's face close to his own. His eyes were on fire.

'Nothing is easy, Pete. But when I give an order it's obeyed without question! Savvy?'

Smith nodded. 'I savvy!'

'We ought to wait until sundown though, boss,' Holden suggested. 'Them redskins don't fight after dark.'

Carter released his grip on the bandanna, then aimed a finger at Holden. 'It won't be dark for hours yet. I'll wager they got a damn sight more ammunition than we have. Am I right?'

All three nodded.

'We have to make a break for it now!'

The Kid leaned closer to Carter. 'Then head for San Remas?'

'Damn right!' Carter acknowledged.

'Good,' the Kid sighed. 'I've kinda had my fill of all this fresh air!'

Carter grabbed a gun from Holden and got on to his knees. He looked at the gunfighter and spoke out of the corner of his mouth.

'You and Pete go and round up four horses.'

This time Billy Holden did not argue or question his boss's orders. This time he and Smith turned and crawled away from him in search of four uninjured mounts.

# SEVENTEEN

The river was narrower nearer the high mesas. Morgan had been here before and knew something of which his younger companion was ignorant. The silver-haired rider steered his mount down through the steep red sand embankment until he reached the river's edge. He reined in, then dismounted just as Taylor reached his side.

'What you doing?' Taylor asked as he swung a leg over the neck of his horse and slid to the ground. He raised an arm and pointed. 'The shooting is thataway. Carter and his men are thataway.'

Morgan smiled. 'Easy, pally. We'll be going thataway soon enough.'

Taylor dropped his reins and scratched his jaw. 'Then how come we've ridden at least a mile in the wrong direction?'

Morgan was still smiling when he moved to the

steep embankment of sand and started to pull brittle brush away with his gloved hands.

'You could give me a hand here, pally.'

'I would if I knew what you were doing.' Taylor crossed the sand until he was standing next to his trusted companion. He accepted the brush and tossed it into the fast-flowing water behind him. 'I know, we're digging a tunnel.'

Morgan stood upright and rested his knuckles on his hips.

'There,' he announced proudly.

Taylor got closer and looked over Morgan's shoulder. His eyes widened in disbelief.

'A boat?'

'Raft,' Morgan corrected.

'OK, a raft,' Taylor shrugged. 'What's it doing here and how come you knew about it?'

Morgan turned and patted the confused Taylor's cheek.

'It's my raft and I put it here.'

Taylor sighed. He was no wiser. 'Why and when?'

Morgan pushed his stronger friend toward the raft. 'That don't matter now. Just help me get it on to the water. We're going sailing.'

Taylor did as he was told. He dragged the raft out of its hiding-place and dropped it just short of the water. He panted and then stared at the amused Morgan. His face begged for answers.

'You ain't telling, are you?'

'Nope,' Morgan said. He bent down and pulled a sand-covered rope free from the raft. 'Tie this to the horses' bridles.'

Taylor again did as he was told. He looped the rope around both their horses' bridles with a firm knot. He gave it a tug and then looked at his friend who was now kicking the raft off the sand and on to the water. He watched as Morgan pulled both their rifles from their saddle scabbards before jumping on to the raft and then sitting down.

'Get on,' Morgan said.

Reluctantly Taylor obliged. Both men sat down with the rifles across their laps. As the current pulled the raft out into its flow they watched as their mounts leapt into the river and swam behind them.

'Can you steer this thing?' Taylor questioned.

Josh Morgan dropped the butt of his rifle into the water to serve as a rudder and then looked at the younger man. 'This will do the job well enough.'

'When we reach the action, what do you reckon our best plan will be?' Taylor was feeling uneasy; the raft was beginning to quicken as the river hauled it along.

Morgan seemed to give it little thought. 'I've always gone for the kill before getting killed kinda plan.'

\*

141

There was no way that Carter's men could bring the horses they had managed to round up any closer. The deadly rifle bullets from the Cheyenne's Winchesters had enough range to reach a dozen yards beyond the large fallen tree trunk that he and the Kid were crouched behind.

They had reached a stalemate. There were so many dead ponies on the opposite riverbank that the Cheyenne braves had been able to use them for cover and avoid shots from the long barrel of the deadly buffalo gun whenever they saw Kid Dynamite level it at them.

Cody Carter knew that he and his youngest hired gun had to make a break for the horses sooner rather than later. But just when he was about to give his instructions to the Kid, they heard the spine-chilling sound of Red Eagle calling out across Blood River.

There had been a lot of war cries mixed with the rifle fire since they had encountered the frenzied warriors but nothing quite like this. Carter gripped the arm of Kid Dynamite.

'What the hell was that?' Carter heard himself ask.

'I don't know, but the shooting's stopped.' The Kid poked his head above the log and stared. None of the Cheyenne was moving. There were now only eleven of them remaining capable of sitting astride their ponies. They were like

142

mounted statues in a long line. 'Look at them, boss!' the Kid gasped in surprise. 'They're begging us to shoot them!'

Carter raised his head and peered over the smouldering tree bark at the sight which had stunned his young henchman.

The only one of the braves to be moving was their chief. Red Eagle held his rifle high above his head and was calling out in broken English.

'Carter! We fight! You! Me! We fight! We finish this now like warriors!'

The Kid glanced at Carter. He could see the benumbed expression carved into his features. The most powerful man in Franklin County was now dishevelled and a pitiful remnant of what he had been only half a day earlier.

'He wants you, boss,' the Kid said. 'He wants a showdown by the looks of it. Just you and him.'

'That's damned obvious, Kid,' Carter sneered. 'My worry is why he wants to tussle with me? I've bin damn good to that critter.'

The Kid looked at the sand at their knees. He only had two sticks of dynamite remaining. He knew that if they were well placed he could wipe out all eleven of the Indians and finally put and end to the bloody battle that had been going on for far too long already.

'Let me try something, boss.'

'Like what?'

The Kid looked deadly serious. 'If I can get to the water's edge without being killed I can throw these two last sticks close enough to them to blow them all to hell.'

'There ain't no way they'd fall for that,' Carter said. 'They've already tasted what dynamite can do. They'd cut you in half before you made a yard from here.'

'I've got another idea.' Kid Dynamite picked up his saddlebags and searched its satchels. He grinned when he found the long coil of fuse.

'How long will that burn for, Kid?' Carter asked as the younger man's expert fingers primed both sticks with the fuse coil.

'Somewhere around two minutes, boss.'

'What do you intend doing with it?'

Kid Dynamite scooped sand away from the edge of the fallen tree trunk and placed the two sticks in the hollow. He then dropped a dozen buffalo gun shells on top of them and covered it with his bandanna before smoothing an inch of sand over his hidden handiwork.

Both men stared at the fuse coil.

'Now we have to lure them over the river and finish this, boss.' The Kid shrugged as he pulled his six-shooter from its holster and held the hammer directly over the end of the fuse. 'Say the word!'

'Do it!' Carter ordered.

The Kid squeezed the trigger. The gun shot into the sand and the gun's firing-pin ignited the fuse.

'Two minutes?' Carter asked.

'Roughly!' Kid Dynamite grinned even more widely. 'Might be only a minute. Maybe less. It's always guesswork.'

'Guesswork? Let's get out of here!' Carter urged, and he frantically started to crawl away from the log with the Kid at his heels.

As Carter closed the distance between the hissing fuse and his awaiting henchmen with the horses he was still curious as to why the Indian chief had turned upon him so suddenly.

Then as he reached Smith and Holden, took the reins from them and hurriedly mounted, he realized that he had not seen Red Eagle's son at any time since the fighting began. His head darted in the direction of the Kid. 'Hey! Have you seen any sign of Red Eagle's boy, Kid?'

Steadying his mount, Kid Dynamite understood what his paymaster meant. 'Ya right. He ain't bin here. Wonder why?'

'Maybe Taylor killed him along with those other braves at the fort, Kid.' Carter looked back at Red Eagle and his remaining men. He raised a hand and waved it mockingly at the Cheyenne.

'Come and get me you back-stabbing bastard!' Carter yelled out at the top of his voice.

'And the chief blames you?' the Kid asked. 'Why?'

Carter beamed when he saw the Cheyenne start to cross the river after them. With each stride of the paint ponies he knew that they were getting closer to the hidden explosives. He looked at his three henchmen in turn.

'Who gives a damn? C'mon!'

The riders turned their horses and spurred. They rode up a high sandy ridge which levelled out at its top. Carter stopped his mount, swung it around and looked down at the chasing Indians. His three men steadied their horses next to him and waited.

'What happens if that dynamite explodes too soon, Kid?' Carter asked his top gun as the youngster held his reins firmly in his hands.

'It won't,' the Kid said confidently.

Kid Dynamite had been pretty close with his presumption as to how much time the length of fuse cord would take to burn down to the dynamite and bullets. His first estimate had been the closest.

No sooner had the mounted Cheyenne braves ridden out of the water and up on to the riverbank than the entire area erupted furiously. The ground shook and the dynamite exploded into a deafening white and red fiery mushroom. Flames swept out from all sides. Acrid smoke swirled and rose slowly upward. Like a Fourth of July fireworks celebration the bullets blistered out in all directions from the deep, hot crater where they had been hidden. If there had been any survivors the buffalo shells would have surely finished them off.

Carter punched a fist into a palm and laughed loudly.

'Our problems are over at last, boys!'

The quartet of horsemen spun their horses around, spurred and rode on in the direction of San Remas.

# EIGHTEEN

The horrific sight which greeted the two rafters as they rounded the bend in the river was something which neither of them could ever have imagined they would see again. They had both witnessed the pointless brutality of war at first hand and thought that its carnage was something they had left behind them on the savage battlefields.

Now as they used their rifle butts to steer the crude raft to the shore, they realized that most men were insane wherever you happened to find enough of them gathered together. They would fight and kill for the most capricious and pointless of excuses. It seemed to the two rafters that nothing had been learned ever since men had first discovered the ability to slay one another.

Decay came swiftly in the baking-hot desert beneath the blazing sun which still had another few hours to go before it eventually vanished beneath the horizon. The scent sickened both men although neither said a word.

The swollen carcasses of horses were like strange islands dotted across the wide river. They were obstacles to be avoided by the rafters.

Both Morgan and Taylor had seen their fill of death during the long war. Now they were seeing more and it turned their guts inside out.

The raft reached the sandbank and Taylor stepped on to the soft ground. Morgan followed a few seconds later.

Taylor grabbed the rope tied to the back of their crude craft and led the two sodden horses on to dry land. The animals shook their heads as the men stared in disbelief at the crater which had destroyed the last of the Cheyenne.

Little remained of either the Indians or their ponies. Just gore and flesh that had already started to attract sandflies.

Taylor shook his head.

'Looks like Kid Dynamite has been busy.'

Morgan ignored the statement. He strolled carefully away from the butchery and then turned to the younger man.

'Four of them rode out, pally.'

Taylor came to his side and nodded when he saw the hoof-tracks in the sand. He looked up at the ridge and then at Morgan.

'They're headed back to town.'

'And Carter's with them,' said Morgan, grimly.

'How do you know that?' asked Taylor.

Morgan aimed a boot toe at one set of hoof-tracks. 'See how deep these tracks are compared to the others, pally? This rider was at least thirty pounds heavier than the others. Only Carter carries that much weight.'

'I'd have figured that out eventually.' Scott Taylor checked his handguns and satisfied himself that they were fully loaded. 'I'll get the horses.'

San Remas did not notice the pair of horsemen who rode tall down its main street towards the large and brightly lit house where Cody Carter and what was left of his gunfighters noisily celebrated their victory over Red Eagle and his warriors. By contrast, the flickering lanterns and storefront lights along the main drag did little to lighten the darkness which had fallen more than an hour earlier. But it allowed those who preferred shadows to move unnoticed for the most part.

It was a dust-caked Josh Morgan and Scott Taylor who reined in outside the telegraph office. Both riders noted that the building had been closed for so long that undisturbed cobwebs covered the door and its frame.

Taylor glanced up at the poles which led away from the side of the wooden office in the direction of the distant Adobe Wells. Their wires swayed in the night air and appeared unimpaired.

Morgan was first to dismount. He looped his reins around the hitching rail, tied them firmly, then stepped up on to the boardwalk. His wrinkled eyes surveyed the street as his companion followed suit.

'Do you think the equipment is still in there?' Taylor asked, vainly trying to see inside the building through its filthy windows.

Morgan shrugged. 'There's only one way to find out, pally.'

Taylor looked at the door. Its upper half was made up of small glass panes. He removed his Stetson, placed it over the pane closest to the keyhole and then elbowed it.

The hat muffled the sound of the breaking glass. Taylor returned his hat to his dark head of hair and reached into the office. His gloved hand found the doorknob and he turned, half-fearing that the door might have been locked. But it opened and the two men went inside.

It took only a few seconds for their eyes to adjust to the dark. In the far corner Morgan found the dust-covered apparatus on a table and sat down beside it. He quickly checked that everything was connected. He wound up the dynamo with some vigour and looked up at Taylor who was leaning over him.

'It's working, pally.'

'See how fast you can send that message, uncle of mine.'

Even though it was years since he had last been required to use the telegraph Morgan began tapping the key with expertise.

Taylor guarded the door as his friend continued to tap out the message informing their Eastern bosses that the bad apple in their barrel was one of their top officers: General Theo Jackson.

'Do you figure they'll believe us that Jackson's the traitor, old-timer?' Taylor asked as his friend completed his work, stood up and walked towards him.

'They will when we deliver the proof in your shirt that verifies our claims,' Morgan replied.

Taylor opened the door to the street. 'If we live long enough to deliver it, you mean.'

Morgan led the way out on to the boardwalk. His eyes were firmly on the large house at the far end of the town. There was a lot of noise drifting out from its open windows as its occupants continued to celebrate.

'You gotta point there,' Morgan said thoughtfully. 'Put those papers in my saddlebags. They'll be safe there. We don't want to risk them getting riddled with bullet-holes or covered in blood, do we?'

Taylor did as he was instructed. He secured the satchel's metal buckle and looked at his companion.

'I'm glad you have faith in my ability.'

Morgan smiled. 'C'mon! We got a party to stomp on!'

Cody Carter had not wasted any time before getting drunk. He sat in the most comfortable chair in the large room, near the open balcony windows, with a decanter of brandy perched on his lap. He warmed a full glass of the expensive liquor in the palm of his left hand and leered at the handful of females Billy Holden had a brought to the house for their general gratification.

'We should have brung the piano-player, boss,' Smith said as he helped himself to the whiskey and allowed two of the Cartwheel's girls to run their fingers over his bruised and aching body.

'And the piano!' Carter laughed before downing another full glass of the brandy.

Kid Dynamite was the quietest of the four men. He had not said a word since they had arrived back. He just brooded in a corner.

Even through his drunken stupor Carter had noticed. He rose from his chair and walked unsteadily to the young gunfighter.

'I give up, Kid. What's wrong?'

The Kid glanced at his boss. 'I'm out of dynamite.'

Carter looked at the sullen features for a few moments and then gave out a bellowing laugh. He

153

rested a hand against the wall and shook his head.

'Is that all?'

The Kid looked hard at his boss. 'I need dynamite. I used up every stick out there protecting your butt, boss. I ain't happy when I ain't got at least a couple of sticks of it on me.'

Carter gave a slight bow.

'I understand, I really do. After all, what's the point of being called Kid Dynamite if you ain't got any dynamite?'

'Are you making fun of me?' The Kid looked angrier than he had back in the desert. 'I killed Red Eagle and his boys out there. Remember that!'

Cody Carter sighed. 'Easy, boy! Go down to the cellar. I have a box of the best dynamite money can buy down there. Grade A. And it's all yours, Kid. Yours to do whatever you want with it. OK?'

Kid Dynamite almost smiled. He glanced around the room and at the females in various stages of undress, and then looked into the red eyes of his employer. He nodded and marched from the room. His spurs rang out as he descended the staircase.

In the shadows Taylor pushed out an arm and stopped Josh Morgan in his tracks just outside the rear entrance to Carter's home. They both hung about by the corner and watched Kid Dynamite run from the stairs to the door to the cellar. He entered.

Both men looked at one another. It was as if they were capable of reading each other's thoughts. They moved as one into the building and to the magnificent staircase. Suddenly Taylor paused and looked back at the door to the cellar.

He gritted his teeth, then indicated to Morgan that he should remain where he was. Morgan nodded and watched as his tall comrade walked back towards the door they had seen the Kid go through.

Taylor drew one of his guns, cocked its hammer and slowly approahced the doorway.

A few feet from the door there were steps leading to a large cold room. Hundreds of bottles of wine, brandy and whiskey were carefully stacked on handmade wooden racks. Taylor guessed that the value of the wine alone was probably more than he could earn in his whole life.

Taylor moved like a panther, silently and with deadly purpose. He looked down to where a single candle burned beside the kneeling Kid.

He focused at the box that the younger man had just opened and its contents.

Deadly contents.

Dynamite. A whole bunch of dynamite.

As Taylor took another step towards the floor of the cellar, the Kid looked up abruptly. His eyes narrowed on the man who was closing in on him.

Taylor saw the Kid's hand move to his six-shooter. He threw himself at Carter's top gun. He landed on the Kid hard and high. Both men rolled over the cold floor and were stopped by the wooden racks of bottles.

The Kid drew his gun. Taylor grabbed the Kid's wrist. They wrestled at the base of the swaying wall of wine. Then the gun exploded and a shot ripped into the younger Kid.

Taylor felt his opponent lurch in agony as hot lead tore into his body from the smoking gun barrel. Then the Kid went limp and slid to the ground. Taylor staggered back to his feet and kicked the gun from the Kid's hand.

He returned to Morgan and looked into his eyes.

'Did you hear the shot?' Taylor whispered.

'Only just, pally,' Morgan answered. 'It was muffled by something.'

Taylor looked down at his blackened shirt. Powder still smouldered upon it.

'Yeah, I'm the something that muffled it.'

They moved through the house until they reached the foot of the wide staircase. They could hear the men and women still enjoying themselves in the large room above them.

Their guns were drawn as they slowly acended.

As if on a mission behind enemy lines they closed in on their prey. Carter was the man who,

156

they could now prove, was responsible for all the mayhem which had occurred within the boundaries of Franklin County.

They had the authority to capture him either dead or alive.

Both men held their guns in readiness of what lay only a few feet above them. What neither of them knew was that in the cellar, a mortally wounded Kid Dynamite was crawling towards the open box of explosives and the burning candle.

# FINALE

Carter stood pouring brandy into his own glass as Smith and Holden lay on the floor and enjoyed the females who had been well paid to service their every need. The laughter was loud and continuous. So loud that it drowned out the footsteps of the two men who walked towards them.

For a few moments none of the people in the big room even noticed that they had uninvited company. They had other, more basic things on their drink-sodden minds.

Taylor and Morgan walked into the light of the lamps and then stopped. Their guns were trained upon the three men.

Carter lowered his decanter and saw them. He raised his glass to his lips, drank, then squinted.

'Who is it?'

Silently Taylor and Morgan took two more steps, then paused. Now the rooom's lights bathed over them.

158

'Pop and his nephew,' Carter smiled. 'Come on in and pick yourselves a whore.'

'My name's not Pop, Carter,' Morgan told him.

Carter staggered a few steps closer. 'I'm drunk, Pop. But not that drunk.'

'What my friend here means is that we ain't who you think we are, Carter,' Taylor added.

'What?' Carter placed his glass on a table and steadied himself. 'OK. Then who are you?'

'My name's Taylor.'

Suddenly the laughter faded. Smith and Holden pushed the females off them and got to their feet.

'Taylor?' Carter's voice shook as he uttered the simple name.

The tall, man nodded. 'Yep, Taylor.'

'But you're dead,' Carter said. 'I seen your body out there at the fort. You were dead.'

Taylor smiled. 'I wondered why you were having a party. I thought it might be 'coz you bettered those Cheyenne.'

Smith and Holden both straightened their gunbelts and moved to either side of their paymaster. The females fled down the staircase.

'We're taking you boys for trial,' Morgan said bluntly.

'No, you ain't,' Carter snarled.

'They can't do this, Mr Carter,' Holden managed to slur. 'Can they?'

'Dead or alive,' Taylor muttered. 'It don't matter

159

none to us which it is. We're taking you in either way.'

'Kill them!' Carter screamed.

Taylor and Morgan moved apart.

Carter went for the gun in the holster hidden under his left arm as his men drew their weaponry. The room shook as the lead flew in both directions.

When the gunsmoke eventually thinned only Taylor and Morgan remained standing. They checked the three bodies. They were all dead.

'Where shall we take them?' Taylor asked his friend.

Morgan holstered his guns and turned. 'Nowhere tonight, pally. We'll pick them up in the morning after we have ourselves some shuteye.'

The two men had barely reached their horses outside the telegraph office when the explosion to end all explosions shook the entire town. Knocked into the sand by the sheer force of it, they managed to turn on the ground and stare in disbelief as the great mansion was blown into a million fragments.

As flames leapt up at the stars Taylor got back up and helped his older companion to his feet.

'How did that happen?' Taylor wondered aloud.

Morgan raised an eyebrow. 'I thought you killed Kid Dynamite in the cellar, pally?'

Taylor scratched his chin. 'Well, he's dead now!'

RTD

CRP